SPELL SPEAKERS
A WHYLAND INTRO NOVELLA

DAY LEITAO

CONTENTS

MEETING FATE

Darian turned fourteen that day. He got something better than a party—a trip to a council of leaders. His village was small and isolated, in a valley surrounded by hills, and he rarely left it. His mother, Bianca, was the leader of the village, and Darian accompanied her for the first time, excited to learn what the leaders discussed. They traveled in a wooden boat, rowing through the currents of streams and then a river. Darian wore pants and a long-sleeved tunic in a light fabric, which kept him cool. On his neck, he wore a necklace his mother had given him with a yellow stone so bright it seemed to shine in the dark. His mother wore its twin.

A whoosh in the sky made him shudder. A lift—a flying machine. It would have been a symbol of progress if it didn't belong to the army, and if the army didn't threaten villages like Darian's.

"Don't worry. They didn't see us," his mother said.

Darian remained alert, but as the hours went by and no other lift was heard or seen, he relaxed. They reached their destination at night. Darian's big brown eyes opened wide, staring at the stars and the bright full moon in a cloudless sky. A hopeful sky. The air was hot and humid as was usually the case this time of the year.

The forest seemed empty. "I don't see anything. Where's the meeting?"

His mother put her hand over her lips and then walked in front of him, making no noise on the ground. He tried to do the same, but he still had no talent for silent steps. They followed the banks of the river, walking for many minutes, until they came to a large waterfall.

She smiled. "You'll have to get wet now."

Darian wondered if they were going to swim, but no. His mother went to the edge of the waterfall, and holding onto the rocks, moved towards its middle, under the main water drop. A protrusion in the rock shielded them from the main waterfall, but the spray was still enough to soak him. Well, it was hot anyway. Soon they came to an opening to a cave. Seven people sat around a fire either directly on the floor or on mats or pillows.

A woman with long, gray hair spoke. "And Bianca's finally here!"

"I'm right on time," his mother replied. "But I apologize if you expected the meeting to start early." She pointed to Darian. "I brought my son."

Her voice was soft, soothing, like from the time she told

him stories and made him sleep. But this time her voice didn't make him want to sleep, it rather just comforted him and made him feel at peace. He wondered if anyone else felt the same.

There were three men and four women. Five, counting his mother, who was the youngest there. They each spoke at a time, talking of the king's army, and how it had been closing in on villages like theirs. Darian knew about it. His village was among the ones that preserved old knowledge and traditions, choosing to remain hidden or isolated with little contact with the larger cities of Whyland. They worshiped the forces of nature, the inner strength, and the strength of mind, personifying different forces with gods and goddesses. Not that it made a difference whether or not they were real. The truth had been broken into little pieces and translated into stories and metaphors because that's how humanity understands the world.

But the king had forbidden magic. Not only that, he accused villages like Darian's of being rebellious and siding with Lylah, who he claimed was a powerful witch. She was in fact a deposed queen, probably already dead. All this talk about an evil powerful witch seemed only to be an excuse to justify extreme actions against innocents. Whyland's army, instead of protecting its people, started to repress them. The time had come to plan a way to resist, a way to survive. That was what the meeting was about. Darian was eager to learn more and to understand what part he could play in all this.

The leaders had similar ideas about union and armed resistance. The woman with the gray hair suggested independence. His mother heard them with calm eyes and attention to each speaker.

Hers was the last turn. She said, "To fight is honorable. Not to fight is also honorable. I know our strength and I know we can resist the army, but I don't know for how long. If we leave our villages and confront the king, we'll be exposing ourselves. More than that, there will be bloodshed." She glanced at Darian so fast it was almost imperceptible, but he noticed it. "And a dreadful future for our children. In the name of what? Pride?" Her voice was almost hypnotic, and Darian could swear it took shape and cast a sparkly, illuminating cloud in the room. "We can resist. But we can resist differently. Our beliefs are deeply rooted in our culture. They are deeply rooted in our way of thinking. We don't need to parade them. We don't need to defy the army, defy the king. We can pretend. We can hide our symbols. We can even pretend we are doing what they want us to do."

"Never!" A voice interrupted her. It was a bearded man, the oldest person there. His interruption was like waking from a pleasant dream. "We are not cowards."

Darian noticed the calm with which his mother looked at the man and how he seemed to have lost his speech. "I agree," she said. "We are not. We are brave. And, yes, we are proud. Our day will come. The king's reign is falling apart. One day we'll be able to fight back. This is not the time. The army has been getting stronger, with more and more flying machines. If one of them decides to burn down our villages, we won't be able to resist. If we want to fight them, we'll need bigger allies and a bigger plan. We'll need to keep meeting and keep planning. Meanwhile, we wait. We bid our time. Our time will come."

The words kept ringing in Darian's ear. *Our time will come.* He realized that was why his mother had brought him. He realized he had a part to play. He took a deep breath. His path, his future, all of a sudden, got clear.

The leaders then voted by casting stones in a basket. A black stone meant waiting. A white stone meant war. His mother had been the only one who had proposed to wait. He was sure there would be an armed conflict. Each of the leaders put a stone in a basket that was placed in the center, with a small hole on the lid, so that nobody saw what was in there. When they opened it, there were seven black stones and one white. His mother's plea had won by a large majority. The power of words, or perhaps the power of the way words were said, was one of the lessons he learned that day.

The gray-haired woman said, "If that's what has been decided, we need to plan our next steps."

Darian's mother said, "I have an idea." She smiled. "A few, in fact. We—" She stopped and perked up, eyes wide. "We need to hide," she whispered.

But it was too late. Sounds could be heard outside the cave. Darian's mother approached him and handed him a dagger. "If necessary," she whispered.

His heart beat fast. He had no idea what was happening and who was coming. A few seconds later, five people traversed the waters of the waterfall. Their clothes were dark blue, the colors of the army, and three had fireguns in their hands. Those weapons, Darian knew, could shoot fire from a distance. They were pointed at him and the leaders.

Darian's mother stepped in front of him. "Stop," she said. "We have more people than you."

"So what?" A woman from the army replied. "We are armed."

"Weapons down," a thunderous voice said as a man in his forties with graying blond hair emerged from the waters.

The soldiers obeyed.

"We don't care what kind of magic or witchcraft you are doing," he said. "I don't give a crap. We are looking for a gang of thieves." He looked at his mother and the other leaders. "Perhaps you'll be able to help us."

The gray-haired woman said, "Do we look like we keep company with thieves?"

"No," the man from the army replied. "But you could have seen something."

The leaders looked at each other, and then at the man. Some shook their heads. Bianca then said, "If we do see anything, is there a way to contact you?"

"We're flying around the area," the man said. "But here." He threw something in her direction. It was a silver disk. She caught it. "If you press it, it will open a communication channel with us. But be careful. And don't travel alone."

"We will, thank you," she said.

The man turned to the other people from the army. "Out of here."

They disappeared as quickly as they had come.

"Liars!" the bearded leader said. "They'll come back with a bigger force. Or worse, they'll follow us. We should have killed them all."

"No," Bianca replied, "he was saying the truth."

The man snorted. "You're going to defend them now? Maybe you told them our location. How could they have found us? We know how much you like men from the army—"

"Shut up!" Even Darian was surprised at his shout. Everyone stared at him. "Maybe they are lying, maybe they aren't. They must have seen one of us. We leave here, and if we're careful not to be followed, we won't have any problems."

The bearded man ignored Darian and turned to his mother. "I'm not going to be lectured by a bad seed like his father."

Bianca was serene. "You don't have to. We were leaving." She turned to Darian. "Let's go."

He followed his mother out of the cave, wondering what the man had meant by bad seed. His father had died before he had been born. Darian knew near nothing about him and had always heard it didn't matter.

THE NIGHT HAD COOLED. Crickets chirped in the distance. As Bianca untied the boat, Darian gathered his courage and asked, "What did he mean? About my father?"

"He was trying to offend you, that's all. When people do that, the best way to irk them is to continue to be calm." She laughed.

"And you really think the soldiers mean no harm?"

"I do, Darian. I saw no ill intent in them. If anything, they would like to protect us. Well, that's their duty."

Bianca stopped, alarmed. Darian looked around. He didn't hear or see anything. She sighed, but still seemed worried. She tossed Darian the silver disk, then whispered, "If something happens. There might be indeed thieves or killers in these woods. I'll go take a look."

"No," he said. "I'll come with you."

She looked at him, seemed to change her mind, and said, "Let's get on the boat and get out of here fast."

They had barely started moving the boat towards the river when a strong boom startled Darian. He looked around to see where it had come from and saw two men coming from the woods.

His mother picked up a large branch from the ground and turned to Darian. "Run. Run away. Go to the river. Save yourself."

He wouldn't do that. He ran towards her instead. Another strong sound was heard. His mother fell backward but got back on her feet. A third man was coming towards them. The men were dressed in brown and black leather and didn't seem to belong to the army. Darian's mother looked at Darian with calm but commanding eyes. "Save yourself."

Darian froze, then remembered the silver disk. He pressed it, unsure of what it would do. He wasn't even sure if these men weren't related to the army, considering one of them had the same kind of weapon the soldiers had.

"Kill her," one of the men said.

"And the boy?" another man asked.

"Also. Or he'll recognize us."

Darian took the dagger his mother had given him, but

everything happened too fast. Fast and slow, because each millisecond would be registered forever in his mind. Bianca swung the branch around her, keeping the men away, and keeping them from reaching Darian. He couldn't move and help her with all the swinging she was doing. The firegun settled it, as another shot reached his mother. She stepped back. Blood dripped from her chest, but she stood her ground and turned to Darian. "Run."

At that moment, one of the men approached her and, with a knife, reached for her neck. She was fast enough to dodge it and to drop him to the ground. But that allowed another man to take aim at her. Darian tried to run towards him, but a different man dropped him to the ground. He had a knife coming in Darian's direction. Another boom and the man fell over Darian. With great effort, Darian pushed the body from him and saw that four of the army people were immobilizing the two other men. His mother lay on the ground and said, "My son, my son, my sons."

A woman sat beside her. "Hush, don't strain yourself."

Darian ran to his mother's side. His sight was cloudy. He held her hand, which was a mess of blood and dirt. He wished he could have done things differently, that he could have saved her, that he could have fought.

Bianca was calm and smiling. That gave Darian hope. She looked at him. "My son, my son. Go to your father. Find him. You need to tell him. Tell him I've always loved him." She breathed out and then no longer in. Her eyes were lost somewhere.

"Mom, mom, mom. Answer me." Tears ran in Darian's eyes.

The woman from the army touched Darian's arm. "She's gone. To a better place."

That couldn't be true. It couldn't. He hugged his mother and sobbed. The light on his necklace faded, and the stone, which had been yellow until then, turned to black.

2

A NEW BEGINNING

Since his return, Darian had stayed with a middle-aged couple, Larah and Saul. Their house, like most houses in the Northern hidden villages, was made of wood with a large common area in the middle and small bedrooms or other rooms surrounding it. Darian occupied one of these rooms, but he didn't want to remain there forever. Perhaps he should go back to his house and live on his own or leave the village and start a new life. He just wasn't sure where. He felt like a burden, a person without a place in the world.

That afternoon the new leader, Leena, visited the couple. Darian pretended to sleep in the bedroom, knowing she'd come to talk about him. He went to the door and rested his ear on it.

"The boy," Leena said. "He can't remain here with you."

Saul said, "Actually, we thought about it. He's helpful and

kind. We could raise him until he's old enough to go on his own. It would be a pleasure."

"I know you're attached to the boy," Leena said. "Who isn't? But this is not our decision. He has a living father."

Darian felt his heart beating.

"Father?" Larah asked. "More like monster. She ran away from him for years. She hid the boy. For what?"

Darian couldn't believe those words.

"This is not my choice," Leena said, "but Bianca's. I made her a promise."

"I see what you're saying," Saul said, "but the boy should be heard in this matter."

His mother's last wish. It made sense now. Darian opened the door. Leena and the couple looked at him, surprised. He said, "Thank you, Larah. Thank you, Saul. I have no words to describe your kindness and love. But my mother's last words," his voice cracked, "were to find my father."

DARIAN LEFT behind everything he had ever known. The trip to the capital, Siphoria, was long. They had walked for days to the Great River and were now on a passenger boat heading south. Darian had been trying to get more information from Leena, but she offered nothing.

"And you won't tell me who my father is?"

"Meet him first, then you can learn what he does."

There was another question—maybe he shouldn't ask it

—about something he'd heard. He had to ask it. "Why would Larah say he's a monster?"

"He and your mother didn't get along in the end. Your mother didn't want to see him. But that doesn't mean he'll be a bad father to you."

"And why didn't my mother ever tell me?"

"She would have told you. One day."

Darian sighed. It wasn't anxiety or fear. He only wanted to know what he was going to do, where he was going to live, what his life would be like. Leena told him none of that. Like the river they followed, he couldn't see where it led. And there was this emptiness in his chest.

He touched the two necklaces with the black stones under his shirt. At least he was doing what his mother had asked. "Tell him I love him," she'd said. A strange thing to say if she'd been hiding from his father for years.

As they reached the Silver River and neared the capital, more and more villages appeared, but they were nothing compared to Siphoria. Darian had never seen anything like it. Streets, houses, and people spread further than his eye could see. There were flying machines in the sky and carts transporting people on the ground. He wondered where he was going in this great city, but they didn't remain there. Instead, Leena led him to the other side of the Silver River, to the King's castle.

"That's where my father works?"

Leena nodded. Darian had never dreamed of being so close to the evil king. Before they reached the castle, two guards approached them.

"Where are you going?"

Leena said, "I need to find Silas Keen. This is his son."

Silas Keen. So that was his name. Darian had heard it, but he couldn't remember when or where, only a sense of dread and fear.

One of the men laughed at Leena. "What did you do to him? You shrunk him?"

"This is not his son," the other man said.

Leena shook her head. "I don't need you to believe me, just take him to Silas."

"General Keen. And he doesn't have any destitute son."

Leena stared at the men. "I will find him. And I will tell him who you are and that you didn't listen to me." Her voice was soft and smooth, not quite as powerful as the way Darian's mother spoke, but still convincing.

The men looked at each other. One of them shrugged. "If you insist."

They grabbed and tied Leena's wrists. She looked at Darian with calm eyes and Darian let the men tie his wrists too.

They were taken not to the castle, but to a large prison. Darian and Leena were pushed through dark corridors. The place smelled of feces, urine, and mold. Solid walls enclosed the cells making it impossible to look inside. The guards opened a door to a cell with four men in it, pushed Darian inside, and closed the door.

He heard Leena. "I need to stay with him."

The door reopened. Leena was pushed inside. One guard said, "We wanted to put you in the women's cell, but if that's what you wish…" He laughed. "Enjoy it."

Darian was thankful but worried. He knew Leena was there to protect him, but he wondered about her safety.

A man with yellow teeth looked in their direction with malicious eyes. "Oooh, pretty boy."

Leena stepped in front of Darian. "You touch a hair of his and you'll be dead."

The man laughed. "Ooooh, I'm scared." Still, he turned around and didn't bother them again.

The other men slept and didn't pay them any attention. There were only two beds. Darian and Leena sat in a corner on the floor. At first Darian thought that they would soon be released, but as the hours went by, he started to worry. He didn't care much for himself. If anything, this dark place matched his state of mind. But he felt bad for Leena even if she remained calm. The guards had taken their belongings, and they had no food. At least they hadn't touched Darian's necklaces. They remained safely hidden under his shirt.

Later that night, the guards threw some food on the floor. The four men kneeled and ate. Leena caught some in her hands and offered it to Darian. "Eat. You'll need your strength. We don't know how long we'll be here."

As hungry as Darian was, he couldn't eat. Not only was the food dirty, he'd been filled with a sense of dread which had closed his stomach. Leena remained calm as if she had been asked to wait in a comfortable room and offered a nice dinner.

A few hours passed. The four men slept. Leena had her eyes closed. Watching cockroaches scurry in and out of holes distracted Darian. The sound of heavy steps came from the hallway. A young man laughed, sounding amused.

Doors to cells opened and closed. "Him—out. Him—out." The voice of the newcomer echoed through the prison. He was picking prisoners to be released. Darian's door opened. In front of him stood a tall and thin young man with a hood covering half his face. If Darian had to guess, he'd say the newcomer was a criminal. The newcomer looked at the four men, then at Darian and Leena.

He turned to the guard. "Who had the stupid idea to put a woman—"

"It was my request, sir," Leena said, with a strange deference.

"He's not talking to you," the guard said.

The hooded stranger tilted his head and looked at her and Darian. He laughed and asked Leena, "What's your crime? Imaginary hocus-pocus?"

"She's not a witch, sir," the guard said. "I mean, maybe she is. But they are here because she claims the boy is Keen's son."

The hooded stranger glanced at Darian, then away. He laughed. "Rising from the dead. Lovely." He took a longer look at Darian, then turned to the guard and said, "Delusion is not yet a crime."

Darian realized he was a teenager, not much older than himself.

The boy turned to Darian and Leena. "You two—out."

Darian was overcome with a sense of relief. Leena, however, replied, "We need to talk to Silas Keen."

The boy snorted. "And you expect him to come to this dump?"

Leena said, "We were brought here, and in good faith,

assume they'll take us to a conference with Silas."

The hooded boy laughed. "Good faith. Look where you are. But if you insist on rotting here…" He looked at the floor and the remaining food on it. "Like this food. Disgusting." He turned to a guard. "What's your problem? This place is filthy. Can't you bring them food in cans?"

"Orders, sir."

The boy rolled his eyes. He took one last glance at Darian before leaving. What a strange place where menacing guards took orders from a criminal teenager. Darian wondered who the boy was.

A few minutes later, two guards opened their cell and took Leena and Darian to a different, empty cell. There were two beds, both hard and without covers. Still, it was a huge improvement. Darian lay awake for a long time, feeling the black stones against his chest, wishing his mother was still alive, wishing they had never gone to that meeting. If only he could have saved her. But it was too late now.

Dreams about dark corridors haunted Darian when he fell asleep. The hooded boy was his father, and he laughed an evil laugh, asking, "How can you think you're my son?"

The next morning, Darian and Leena remained in their cell. No food was given to them. Darian began to think he was going to die there. He was not sure if he cared. He was not even sure if he wanted to meet this mysterious father. After a couple hours, two men opened their door. They wore the army's dark blue under long overcoats. Their boots were shiny and clean. They looked like commanders. One of them asked Leena, "Are you sure you want to go on with this farce? I could set you free."

"I can go—if you take the boy to Silas."

The man replied, "We're taking you two. But the punishment is harsh for impersonators. You may regret this."

"That's my problem, isn't it?" she said.

The men put a hood on Darian. He couldn't see anything. He was pushed through the hall and then into a vehicle. They closed the doors behind him. Based on the sounds, he guessed it was being pulled by horses, which was rare for a moving vehicle in a city. Leena untied Darian and pulled his hood off.

She said, "I'm leaving now. You'll soon meet your father. Don't forget us."

"But I don't..." he wasn't sure what he wanted to say. "What if I don't want to stay?"

She smiled. "Boy, this is your path. Do the best you can with it."

His eyes were filled with tears and his vision was blurry. It wasn't that he was attached to Leena but attached to his life, and to whom he had been until then. She was his last link to all of that. Without her, he'd be left in a dark carriage, not knowing where he was going.

"I should meet my father then have a choice."

She shook her head. "That's not how it goes." She took a pin and worked on the lock of the door. She turned to Darian. "Put your hood back on or they might be angry." She laughed. "They'll be scared enough that I escaped." She opened the door.

They were moving fast. She couldn't possibly... She

jumped before Darian finished his thought. Darian watched her roll onto the grass, get up, and wave to him. He had no other goodbye.

When they stopped, Darian put his hood back on. The men cursed when they realized Leena was gone. They pushed Darian up many steps and through many echoing corridors before removing his hood and telling him to sit.

He was in a room with some wooden chairs and a table with green varnish. Although simple, the furniture was elegant and of good quality. The floor was made of wood, and it was clean and shiny. Daylight-looking light came from the ceiling. Darian knew the ceiling was not actually translucent, it was just the way they lit things in the capital. Still, it was interesting for him to see that for the first time. He figured he was in the castle or a fine house. He also figured, or at least hoped, that he was going to meet his father. A long time passed. One, two, three hours… Darian was not sure.

A man outside said, "What a waste of time." Someone opened the door. A man with a short beard, in his late thirties, dressed in flamboyant green velvet with a blue cape stood in the doorway. Two men accompanied him. The man with the blue cape saw Darian and froze as if he'd seen an apparition. He turned to the two men and said, "Go, I'll be fine here."

The man closed the door behind him and stared at Darian. "Is this possible?"

3

WITHIN WALLS

The man was Darian's father: Keen. Darian was
relieved he would not be killed or put back in
prison, but he couldn't muster any special feeling
towards the man in front of him. Keen was a stranger. He
asked Darian many questions about his mother and his life.
They kept talking as they had a late lunch. Darian explained
where he had grown up and how his life had been, but
avoided details about hiding from the army and conspiring
to resist the king. Keen said he'd thought Darian and Bianca
had died many years before, but that he had recognized
Darian at once.

"You look just like her," Keen said, staring at him with a
mix of admiration and wonder.

At the mention of his mother, Darian almost told him
she'd said she loved him, but somehow it didn't sound right.
Darian also learned that his father was the main
commander of the king's army, a piece of information that

knotted his stomach and explained his sense of dread when he'd heard his name.

DARIAN SAT in his windowless room illuminated by the fake translucent ceiling, feeling a sense of emptiness. He also felt like a traitor to his people, to his mother, being among the people against they fought. His only consolation was remembering the soldiers who'd saved him and tried to save his mother. There was still some good in the king's army. His other, less comforting consolation was his suspicion that it was one of the village leaders who had ordered his mother's death. When evil and good are muddled, it's easier to side with the less than honorable one. Or at least to make excuses.

His door was opened and a tall boy with brown hair and eyes dressed in the army's dark blue entered. His clothes were clean, new, and well fitted. He had the air of an army leader despite his boyish face. He looked at Darian. "Incredible. You did rise from the dead."

Darian recognized the voice. It was the boy from the previous night, but what a difference. He had none of his previous criminal looks.

"You're the one who told Keen about me, aren't you?" Darian asked. "I wanted to thank you."

The boy laughed. "Are you crazy? I let you spend the night in that horrible place." He looked at Darian and became serious. "I had no idea. I couldn't have imagined it. I never thought I'd see you alive."

"Who are you?" The question escaped Darian's lips before he could think of something more fitting to say.

The boy raised his eyebrows and laughed. "You don't know who I am?" He waved his arms, put his hands on his chest and made an exaggeratedly sad face. "What a dreadful thing to say. Can't you recognize the awesome looks?" He sat and smiled. "But hey, I'm in a good mood and I'll give you a tip. I'm Sian."

He looked at Darian as if expecting some grand reaction. As Darian hesitated, the glee in Sian's eyes faded. Darian looked down, then back at the boy. "I'm sorry, I'm not from here. I'm not acquainted with the important people in the army. Or the castle."

Sian stared at him, his face surprised and his jaw tense. "You never heard my name. Never?" His voice shook, and he was trembling.

Darian didn't like to see him so upset. "Uh, maybe, it's possible—"

Sian got up and snorted. "*Possible.*" Did he have tears in his eyes? He looked away. "Thanks for letting me know." He left and slammed the door behind him.

Darian felt bad for him, but then, maybe it was just Sian's sense of pride which had been hurt. The previous night, at the prison, Sian had come in all-powerful, telling everyone what to do, and picking and choosing criminals to be released. Perhaps it was just that Sian had a high rank in the army and was offended that for once someone didn't recognize him. That, of course, didn't explain why he seemed so hurt.

THE BED WAS comfortable and Darian had had a good dinner, but he was restless. He missed his mother, his village, his life. He touched his necklaces. They felt cold and dead. He wondered if they would ever work again.

The enclosure of the castle suddenly felt oppressive. If only he could go outside and look at the sky, look at the trees, step on the grass and feel the earth beneath him.

It was late at night, but he couldn't fight the urge to go outside. The hall had many doors, but he paid attention to where he was going to make sure he would find his way back. He came to three more halls and more doors. If only he were in a small house. The castle felt cold and empty. He tried to think where to go but that was pointless, since he didn't know those halls or where they led. Perhaps it was better to relax and follow his intuition.

He chose a hallway. As he walked in it, a door opened, and he collided with someone. It was a girl in a summer dress. She had dark hair and eyes and was surprised.

"You're not allowed here," she said. The girl was young like him.

"I'm sorry, I'm lost. I'm just trying to go outside."

She laughed and rolled her eyes. "It's not me, it's the rules. These are royal quarters." She looked at him. "Who are you?"

"I got here yesterday. I mean, today. I'm general Keen's son."

She squinted and looked at him up and down. "What's your name?"

"Darian."

"Ah. Makes sense."

He thought she was going to say hers, but she didn't. "And you?"

"Me what?"

"Your name?"

She laughed. "You don't know who I am?"

Her tone was amused, but Darian remembered Sian's extreme reaction and feared offending her. "Please, don't be angry. I'm not from here, I don't know anything about the castle, anything about the army, the king, the—"

"Fine, fine, fine," she interrupted. "No problem. I'm Cayla."

She looked at him waiting for a reaction. Darian sighed. "I'm sorry. I really don't know anything about names here."

Cayla squinted and stared at him. "You sure?"

"I'm sorry."

She waved her hand and laughed. "Oh, don't worry. I didn't know who you were either. See?" She smiled. There was something cheeky about it. "My father works in the castle." She shrugged. "So I live here."

Darian knew there were attendants, servants, and cooks in the castle. The girl was dressed simply enough that he figured she must be the daughter of one of these workers. He was relieved to find someone normal like him.

"Can you tell me how to go outside?"

"Well, of course. You..." She pointed to the direction behind Darian, but then stopped. "Were you going some-where? To the city or something?"

"No. I just wanted some fresh air, and, I don't know, step on the grass and see something alive and green."

"That's it?"

"Why? Is wanting to see the night sky unusual here?"

She laughed and shook her head. "No, but I was going to a garden. Just to go outside. There's nothing there really, just trees, and—"

"That would be perfect."

"Follow me then. But don't tell anyone."

"Why? I'm not supposed to go there?"

"Most people aren't. They're private gardens. But I have the key." She winked.

"I don't want you to get in trouble."

She rolled her eyes. "I was going there anyway. Don't think you're special. You can come with me if you want, otherwise I'll leave you to find your way in this maze."

Cayla turned around and started walking. Darian paused for a moment, deciding whether to follow or not. She hadn't exactly asked him nicely. Well, he would be lost on his own. He hurried and caught up with her. They came to a tiny door leading to a small winding staircase, which led to another door. She opened it with a key. It led to a garden with many trees. High walls encircled it. Despite the enclosure, Darian was happy to see the sky.

Cayla climbed a tree faster than he could have imagined anyone climb, especially in a dress. The girl took a fruit and started to eat it.

Darian wanted to make some conversation. "What is it you're eating?"

"Calis," she said, from the top of the tree. "The trees

come from Arlenia, the kingdom north of us. If you want one, come and get it."

She said it as if she was daring him. It was a bit childish. He was past the age of climbing trees. Still, he climbed it. The branches were farther apart than he had predicted, but he concentrated and continued because the girl looked at him as if she didn't think he could make it.

He didn't even want to eat anything, but he took a fruit anyways and bit into it. It was bitter.

Cayla laughed. "You took a green one." She jumped from the tree and landed gracefully on the floor below him. "I have a good one here, but you have to jump."

Darian lay on the branch and looked at the sky. He wasn't going to be ordered around by a silly girl. In a way, it was good to have some peace.

After a few minutes, Cayla climbed back up beside him. "I bring you here and now you're going to ignore me?"

"No." He felt bad because he didn't want to offend her. "I was just… resting, thinking."

Cayla squinted. "I think you're afraid to jump."

He shrugged. "I can climb down."

"Do what you want, but don't ignore me. It's rude." She jumped down.

He climbed down after her and found her on another tree, resting against the trunk, looking at the sky. He followed and did the same on a thick branch beside hers. Perhaps climbing was childish, but it felt good to relax among the trees. There was something comforting in the darkness of the night and the stars. For the first time since his mother had died, he smiled.

Someone shook Darian awake. It was his father.

"Son, wake up. You'll start your training today."

Darian's eyes took a while to adjust to the brightness from the ceiling. "Training?"

"For the army. You're my son. Your brother will oversee your training."

Wait. What? "Brother?"

"Didn't he come see you last night?"

It hit him. So that was why Sian had been so upset. "You mean Sian? He's my half-brother?"

Keen frowned. "Of course not. He's your older brother. A year and a half older. Your mother never mentioned him?"

That definitely explained why Sian had been so hurt.

4

TRAINING

A soldier walked Darian to the military academy. He tried to make sense of the new information, new family, new brother, and new life. The academy was on the other side of the river, near Siphoria. He could see the city with its many buildings, busy streets, and cars moving on rails taking people around it. The military academy was by a high tower, housing living quarters and the administration of the army. Darian was given simple blue pants and a shirt, and told to go to a training arena. Other trainees like him sat on long benches surrounding a flat platform. In the center stood Sian and an older man. Darian wished he could apologize to his brother, say something, but he didn't know how he could do it in front of all these people.

Sian laughed. "Well, well, here's the mommy's boy. And late." He glared at Darian.

"Keen woke me up. You want to complain to him?"

Sian raised his eyebrows. "Daddy's boy as well?" He laughed. Some trainees also laughed. "Arriving on time is your responsibility."

Right. Sian was in the mood to humiliate him. Darian just hoped it would make up for learning that his mother had never mentioned his name. Perhaps not quite. Still, Darian didn't say anything.

Sian addressed everyone. "We have many hand-to-hand combat techniques. But today we'll focus on wrestling." He turned to Darian. "Can you wrestle?"

"No."

Sian smiled. There was something snarky and unsettling about it. "Of course. Be thankful I'm here to teach you. Come to the center."

Darian did as he was told.

Sian looked him up and down. "What is this? Who gave you those rags?"

Darian shrugged. Indeed his clothes seemed old and used, but he didn't really care.

Sian laughed. "Oh. I forgot. You're used to it."

Darian ignored what his brother said, hoping it would irritate him even more.

Sian said, "Come here and drop me on the floor."

"I told you I don't know how to wrestle."

Sian crossed his arms. "It'll be easy for you. I won't use my arms." He spread his legs apart. "And I won't move from this spot."

Darian took a deep breath. It was better to do what Sian wanted. He stood in front of his brother, who stared at him and didn't move. Darian didn't want to move either.

"What? Afraid?" Sian asked.

No. Untrained. It was better to try to attack Sian. Darian tried to tackle his brother, but Sian tripped him before he was within reach. Darian fell backwards on the ground.

Sian laughed. "Oh, that's too bad. No wrestling for you today. You can go to the study room and read. You'll be back later for weapon training."

Darian walked away. He was actually relieved. Later, when he returned to learn about fire weapons, his brother was not there.

Darian had difficulty, and some trainees laughed at him, but he didn't care. In a way, he wanted to learn to fight. If he had known how when he and his mother had been attacked, he could have saved her. But it was too late now.

He returned to the castle exhausted. His father came to see him and asked how the training was going. Darian described it without getting into specifics and said nothing about the incident with Sian. Keen nodded, then left satisfied. Darian had the odd feeling that his father was less interested in him and more interested in his training. This strange man, who claimed to be his father, acted like a superior, not a family member. Maybe things would change. Later, Darian wondered if he would see Cayla again, but she didn't show up.

On the second day of training, Sian again challenged Darian, and again dropped him to the floor. Darian left and was back for the afternoon.

At night he saw his father but he didn't see Cayla. He started to think the girl who reminded him of home had been a dream. At least now he knew how to leave the castle, and he could walk outside the walls where his feet could touch the grass and he could feel the beauty of nature and the strength of the universe. Of course, it would be nicer to do this with a friend, even if he had to do it in a secluded garden.

The following days of training continued like the first two. Darian never wanted to fight his brother, but Sian's teasing was crueler when he refused, and Darian found it better to comply. He never got a chance to see his brother alone and talk to him. Perhaps it was better to let Sian drop him on the floor, make him a little happy, then go to a room where he could stay alone with his thoughts.

At night, Darian's father continued to check on his progress. Darian talked about weapons and strategy, but avoided saying anything about the wrestling. His father would nod and leave. This was their only contact. The days passed and Darian still saw his father as a stranger.

One night, when Darian was almost asleep, he heard soft knocks on the door, and got up to open it

Cayla was there. "Up for a night adventure? Or too tired?"

He smiled. "Never tired."

She stared at him. He realized he wasn't wearing a shirt. She said, "Nice necklaces."

He shuddered, but then remembered few people in Whyland knew what twin necklaces were and what they did.

"Thanks. Let me get dressed." He walked in and put on the first shirt he found.

They walked again to the garden encircled by walls. This

time they talked. He told her about his village, leaving out details about their beliefs or their plans to resist the king and his army. She told him about life in the castle and how she spent her days studying with her younger sister and a teacher. Darian felt relaxed and at ease.

DARIAN ARRIVED LATE at the training academy. To his surprise, his brother wasn't waiting for him, but sitting and watching. Darian was happy he'd have a chance to talk to him.

He sat by Sian and said, "Listen, I'm sorry. I'm really sorry. I don't know why our mother wouldn't—"

Sian didn't look at him. "She's not my mother, little brother."

"Our father said—"

"If he meant Bianca gave birth to me, he was right. But that doesn't make her my mother."

"I'm sorry."

Sian looked at him and chuckled. "Save your sorry and pity for those who deserve it."

"Fine. But you could stop insulting me. I don't see why you're doing it."

Sian stared at him, then sighed. "Oh, well, that's what I get for looking after my little brother. I wasn't expecting thanks or deep gratitude, mind you. But if I bother you so much, I can stop overlooking your training."

"What training? I haven't learned a single thing from you."

Sian tilted his head and looked in his eyes. "How would you like to start? Fasting for two days? Not eating until you drop me to the floor? If you want, I could train you just like I was trained. Is that what you want?"

"I'd like to learn how to fight. You could show me something." Darian thought he could stroke his ego. "You are the best at it, aren't you?"

Sian shrugged. "So what? I haven't heard of a single war won in hand-to-hand combat." He pointed to his head. "You win here."

Sian got up and left.

Darian was sorry to see his brother go. He turned to watch the training. Everyone stood in a circle while two trainees fought. Darian had never reached this stage in the training. One trainee immobilized the other on the floor and punched him. Now, punching as far as Darian knew, wasn't part of wrestling. The trainer, instead of stopping it, encouraged it. Blood poured from the nose of the boy being punched.

Darian ran into the middle of the ring. "Stop it! He's already immobilized!"

Everyone stared at him, including the boys who had been fighting.

The trainer frowned. "You'll take his place then."

Darian wanted to protest, say he'd tell his father or brother, but he didn't want to sound like a scared boy. The truth was, he had never learned any fighting when he lived in his village or since starting the academy, but he had no choice.

"Fine," he said.

The boy was tall, muscular, and probably weighed twice as much as Darian. They faced each other in the circle. Darian stood still, paid attention, and dodged whenever his opponent approached. He kept dodging, but the boy eventually dropped him to the ground. Darian wasn't afraid of the punch, wasn't afraid of losing the fight, of losing a tooth or getting a purple eye. He was afraid of something else.

At that moment, lying on his back, he remembered the day his mother had died, how he'd been dropped to the ground, and how the man above him had lowered a knife. But there was no knife coming towards him. It was a fist. And yet, it reminded Darian of that day. He wanted to scream, to turn back time, to have been stronger.

Sometimes he wished he hadn't been saved, that the knife had stabbed him, that he had followed his mother to wherever she'd gone. He wondered if enough punches could do the same. But the fist never hit his face. Someone lifted the boy off him.

Sian.

He laughed. "That was a lovely display. Thank you for putting the mamma's boy in his place."

"I didn't finish," the boy said.

"You're finished now. You won. We don't hit a foe on the floor."

"That's not what our trainer says."

Sian glanced at the trainer. "Of course."

The trainer shook his hands. "Your father's orders."

Sian smiled. "It strengthens character, doesn't it? I should know, as my character is so strong. Not honorable, mind you, but strong."

He saw the boy with the bleeding nose and told the trainer, "Take him to a doctor." He had the same effortless command Darian had heard in the prison. The trainer obeyed.

Sian looked at the trainees. "You all. You'll fight together. Not against each other. We're brothers. And sisters. There will be girls if you go to piloting and strategy. So let's respect each other." He looked at the boy. "You're suspended."

"You can't do that," the boy said.

"Yes, I can," Sian replied.

Darian felt bad for the boy. "It's not his fault. It's the trainer's."

"Blaming your superiors is cowardice. You can make choices," Sian said.

That was true. And it was true, despite appearances, that his brother had something in him that was honorable and even idealistic.

"My choice," the boy said, "is to prove that I'm the strongest. We're not all brothers. I don't have a daddy or a brother to defend me. I won't get a command position just because I was lucky to have a father who's the main general."

Sian laughed. "Jealous, pal? I can expel you from the army. Would you like that?"

"If you're fair like you're pretending to be, you know I shouldn't be suspended or expelled."

"Unlucky you. I'm not fair and I have no intention to pretend to be."

"You aren't," the boy replied. "You are a dirty hypocrite who associates with the lowest people in Siphoria."

Sian smiled smugly. "Got a problem with that?"

"I don't think a wannabe general should be spending time with dirty men and women."

In one second, Sian had the boy on the floor, throwing punch after punch. "Who's dirty? Who's dirty? Do you want to repeat that?"

The boy spit blood. "No."

Sian got up and addressed everyone. "Don't make assumptions about me or who I keep company. Training is dismissed for today."

Darian tried to reach his brother, but he had walked away too fast. He wondered what had angered him so much. Sian's feelings seemed to bottle up under a cool façade. He wondered what those feelings were.

CAYLA KNOCKED on his door at night. Darian had forgotten it. He got dressed quickly. As they walked outside, he told her about his brother. She said she'd heard he went to the worst parts of Siphoria, but had no idea what exactly he did there. Darian thought his brother was perhaps helping small criminals like he'd done in the prison, but he didn't say anything, because he didn't want her to know he had been arrested.

He also told her about the teasing and wrestling.

"Sian likes to annoy people," she said, and then smiled. "But we could practice."

"What?"

"Wrestling. I've always wanted to learn it. I read a book and tried to do some moves—"

"But you're a girl."

She squinted. "So what?"

"It's just…" Even Darian wasn't sure why he'd said that. "You'd do better with a distance fighting technique."

She nodded. "I train in that as well. But immobilizing people could be useful, no?"

"Maybe."

"You think I'm weak? It's not about strength, it's about technique."

She was tall, perhaps even a bit taller than him, and strong for a girl. He didn't want to imply that she was too weak to wrestle him. "And you can show me some technique?"

She walked to a flat place where the grass was soft. "Come here."

He stood before her. She pulled one of his arms, pushed his opposite shoulder, and put one of her legs behind his, as if to trip him. She smiled. "See?"

"I guess that's a perfect move against someone who won't fight back."

She squinted. "It's basic. What did you expect? Do you know anything better?"

"We can start with basic." He walked towards her and tried the same move, but she pulled his hand and dropped him. It was unfair and annoyed him.

She laughed. "I got you."

He saw her bright eyes and smile and his annoyance

disappeared. "Fine. If I'm allowed to defend myself, I'll defend myself, but don't complain."

"We're learning. I'm not going to complain."

She used the same move on him again, but he blocked it and didn't fall. He came up with a different move, based on what he'd seen, and they practiced. He let her drop him a few times and sometimes she dropped him on her own. He also made sure to drop her a few times; otherwise she'd complain he was going easy on her. In a way, it was good practice—being both beginners, they were able to learn the moves slowly.

At the end, they lay down and laughed. Cayla's hair was a dirty tangle of grass and earth—Darian's was probably dirty as well—but neither of them cared.

DARIAN DIDN'T SEE Sian the next day, nor the trainer or boy who had meant to punch him. They didn't practice any more fighting or wrestling, but learned about weapons and strategy instead.

His father checked on him as usual. Later that night, Darian got ready to practice with Cayla. When she knocked, he opened the door right away.

Cayla laughed. "For once you don't look like you're half asleep."

"Cause I knew you'd come."

They tiptoed through the hallways to the garden where they practiced a little. When Cayla asked why Darian wanted to fight, he told her about his mother's death, how he had watched the men kill her, how he hadn't been able to defend her, and about the guilt he felt because of it.

She listened, then passed her fingers through his hair. Her hands were soft and her eyes kind "What did she ask you to do?"

He looked down. "Run."

"Would she have liked to see you hurt?"

"No, but—"

"She defended you and saved you. I think that's what any mother would have done. If there were three against the two of you—"

"Had I been really good—"

"You don't know that. You don't know why this happened, but it was her day to die, and your destiny to survive her. Maybe there's a reason. And you're here in the castle now, with a new life…"

"I'm not sure I like my life."

She pulled her hand away from his hair and looked down. "I thought you liked…"

"Oh, don't get me wrong. I like to spend time with you. It's the only thing that keeps me happy. You're my best friend."

Cayla looked away, then looked at him. For the first time, she looked vulnerable and sad. "You know, I never met my mother. She was killed in the confrontation against Lylah." She looked up. "I'm going to kill her, you know? That's my destiny. To destroy Lylah."

Darian understood her feelings of anger and desire for revenge, and didn't tell her that Lylah was probably already dead. He only nodded.

"I don't want to compare my story to yours, or to ask for pity… but it must be good to have known who your mother was, to have spent time with her."

Darian closed his eyes. "It was."

He lay on the grass, Cayla beside him. "You don't feel like training today, I guess."

"No."

"What do you want to do?"

"Look at the stars."

"Darian, how old are you?"

Funny how it was the first time she had asked him. "I turned fourteen five months ago." He wished he could forget that day. "You?"

She laughed. "You're younger than me! I'm fourteen and seven months."

"Just a little. And it doesn't matter, does it?"

She was silent for a moment. "I guess it doesn't. And you really don't know who I am?"

"Why? Did you give me a fake name?"

She laughed. "That's my real name. You don't care who my father is?"

"Why? You want to talk about him?"

She hesitated. "Not really." Then she laughed. "I have to get used to the idea that you're younger than me! And shorter."

"Just a little."

He lay with his back on the grass, staring at the sky. Cayla turned sideways and rested her head on her hand, her long dark hair touching the ground. "But it doesn't matter, right?"

"Nothing matters." He reached out with his hand and touched her hair. It was thick and soft. She looked at him with soft dark eyes. For a moment he thought he wanted to kiss her, but he pushed the thought away. He didn't want to lose Cayla as a friend. But still, he passed his hands through her hair as they looked at each other. She was so pretty. Just looking at her made him happy.

They walked back to the castle. Darian now knew his way, so she left him at the beginning of his hallway. As he walked to his room, a person moved out of the shadows.

Sian.

"Hello, little brother."

"I thought you lived in the military complex."

"I do. Builds character. Of course, you don't need any of that. But this is not why I'm here. You're playing with fire, little brother. You need to be more cautious."

"About what?"

Sian shook his head. "It's worse than I thought."

"Whatever you want to tell me—tell me."

"The girl. Do you have any idea what you're doing?"

Darian was puzzled that his brother would have a problem with that. "She's my friend."

"Friends don't spend time alone together in the evening."

"Maybe if I didn't train all day—"

"Whatever. But be careful. Nobody can catch you."

"Why?"

Sian snorted. "I don't know if you're a mad genius, if you're dumb, or if you're just pathetic. You don't know who she is?"

"Her father works in the castle."

He nodded. "Indeed. That's a way to put it. And what is it you like about her? Her entitled attitude? Her bony face?"

"You won't insult her." He had raised his right hand in a fist.

Sian took Darian's hand and lowered it. "Chill. You like her. Great for you. If she feels the same, even greater, but please be careful."

"She's my friend, that's all."

"Thanks for clarifying: you are pathetic."

"You like to offend me, I got it. Anything else?"

"Her father. He won't be happy if he hears she's been lying on the grass with you."

"What are you suggesting?"

"Nothing. But her father might suggest something."

"Who's her father?"

Sian rolled his eyes. "I'll leave that up to you to figure out. But please try to find a more discreet place to... be friends. Or something bad could happen."

Darian didn't like his brother's tone or what he was suggesting. "Is this a threat?"

"Of course not. It's a warning." He patted Darian's shoulder, then took a deep breath. "I won't be around for the next few days. Please make sure you stay alive and unharmed. Keep your head down and you will be fine. I think your wrestling days are over." He mussed Darian's hair. "Bye, little brother."

What had his brother meant? Her father? Who could her father be? Cayla wore simple dresses, walked barefoot, and climbed trees. She was fierce, free, and spontaneous. But then, she did also spend her time studying. Maybe her father was someone important. That could be. He would ask her about it the next evening.

But Cayla didn't knock on his door the next evening, or the following evening, or the following after that. Finally, on the fifth day, Darian received a message. It said, *Sorry. I can't see you. People are watching.*

Darian crumpled the paper in his hands. This had to have his brother's hand. It was weird. Sometimes he thought Sian was kind and even cared about him, but sometimes, he only saw hatred and jealousy. And why? Because he had lived with their mother? Because his father had asked him to live in the castle? All things which Darian had no control over. He tried to understand his brother, but sometimes it was hard. Why keep him from seeing Cayla? What difference did it make to him?

Darian's only solace is that he started making friends at the academy. He realized people had avoided him in the beginning for fear of his father and brother, but having learned he was, for the most part, normal, were able to relax in front of him. But he still missed Cayla. She came to his thoughts often, especially when he was alone. It was getting hard to think about her as only a friend. He remembered her lying beside him, couldn't help the feelings that came to him, and couldn't stop thinking about it.

5

THE BALL

"I can't dance," Darian said. His father had just announced that the family had been invited to a ball at the castle the following evening to honor visitors from Arlenia.

Sian laughed. It was one of the few dinners he had been to. "Don't you do some hocus pocus dancing? For magic or something? Maybe you could adapt it."

Keen gave a hard glance towards his older son.

Sian looked down. "It was a joke."

"It is not funny," Keen said. "You know we're fighting against it."

Sian repressed a chuckle. "Because magic is so threatening."

"Laugh all you want. It menaces peace."

Sian sat up. "But we're here to talk about the ball, right?" He pointed to Darian. "I can teach him to dance."

Darian glared at his brother. "Like you taught me how to wrestle?"

Keen ignored Darian and nodded to his older son. "Do that, Sian. Find him a dance teacher. And a tailor. You two must look like princes."

"I will, father," Sian said.

Keen nodded. "Very well. You are dismissed."

Darian hadn't finished eating, but he left. Sometimes his father spoke to him as if he were speaking to an inferior in the army. It was still jarring.

As the boys walked out the door, Sian said, "Talk about last minute invite. How inconsiderate." He looked at Darian. "You don't really need me to teach you how to dance, do you?"

"Of course not."

"Well, since you don't know anything, I'll give you a tip: hold the girl's hand and do whatever she wants. That's apparently also great advice for a relationship."

"What do you know about it?"

"Nothing. I can't settle my heart." He put his hand on his chest and made an exaggeratedly sad face. "So many choices." He smiled. "I'm kidding. Love is for fools. But we could go to Siphoria tomorrow. I'll get you a nice suit."

Darian hadn't forgotten Sian's hand in separating him from Cayla. "There's a tailor in the castle. And I have to train tomorrow."

"I don't know if you noticed, but it was an order."

"What? Now you're going to tell me what to do?"

"Not me. Our father. You can disobey him at your own

risk. But I was told to get you a nice suit and I will. Not a piece of crap from the tailor here."

"And I can just skip training?"

"You'll train with me. In Siphoria." He laughed. "Don't forget I'm still in charge of your training, little brother."

THE NEXT DAY Darian waited for Sian in his room. His brother arrived wearing a brown overcoat. Darian wore his army uniform.

Sian laughed when he saw him. "You're not going to Siphoria like that, are you?"

"I don't have any other clothes."

"That's a tragedy! Is that why you meet your friend in your night clothes? I thought you were going for an intimate look."

"I don't care about clothes."

"Girls do, little brother."

"What do you care about it? The only girl I was friends with was Cayla and you separated us."

Sian nodded. "Of course. I'm protecting you. You need to find a secret place to meet, that's all."

The matter-of-fact confession surprised Darian. "So it *was* you. What did you *do*?"

Sian lowered his voice. "I sent her a note. I told her people were watching. That was all. It was the same thing I did to you. I'm a nice future brother-in-law."

"Sian, we aren't—"

"I know you aren't together yet. These things, they take time, patience, persistence, resilience, whatever. I'm going to confess I have no clue. I don't have time for that nonsense."

"So don't try to meddle in stuff you don't understand."

Sian smiled. "So now you admit you're interested in her? You figured who she is?"

"How could I? Thanks to you I never saw her again."

Sian raised an eyebrow. "Really? I thought you knew."

Darian took a deep breath and spoke with the calmest voice he could muster. "Aren't you going to tell me?"

Sian chuckled. "Are you kidding me? And ruin the surprise?"

The calm was gone. "Surprise? How?" Darian thought for a moment. "Wait. Is she going to the ball?"

"I don't have foresight abilities, and if I did, it would be forbidden. But yes, there's a good chance she'll be there. One more reason to get a terrific suit." He looked him up and down. "And some civilian clothes to walk in the city. I'll get you some."

IT WAS the first time Darian walked inside the city, away from the military complex. His overcoat was ugly, but it was true that it allowed him to blend in more easily. Many people, from all walks of life, knew his brother—soldiers guarding the city, merchants, passersby... As much as Darian was angry with Sian for separating him from Cayla, there was something pleasant about walking alongside him. Darian was reminded that he still had a bit of his family intact, that he wasn't alone in the world. In a way, he hoped he could get to know his brother, and that they could one day bridge their differences. Of course, his brother would first have to stop meddling with Darian's friendships.

At the tailor, there were too many choices of fabrics, styles, and things Darian had never seen. Sian insisted, and Darian let him choose his outfit. But then his brother chose a red velvet suit: exaggerated and flamboyant just like Sian. Nothing like Darian. He would have picked something black or blue.

Sian chose a dark brown suit for himself and tried to justify the choices "People don't know you, so you'll want to make a good first impression. Plus, it doesn't hurt to look dashing for your friend."

"That's all nice and neat, but I would rather spend time alone with her and make an impression without worrying about how I'm dressed."

"I understand. I just want you alive. That's all. Unlike some people, I care about my family."

"Are you talking about our mother?"

His smug smile left his face. "We don't share a mother. And I was talking about me."

As the time for the ball approached, Darian started to think that letting his brother choose a suit had been a terrible idea. That red was too flashy. Worse, the suit looked hot. He wished he could hide in his bedroom or that Cayla would knock on his door wearing whatever. He wanted to lie on the grass with her, touch her hair, let her touch his.

An actual knock awoke him from his daydream, and he ran to the door wondering if it was her.

It wasn't.

It was Sian. "I know being late is fashionable and makes an impression, but our father wants us there now."

Darian got dressed quickly. When he came out, his brother looked him up and down with a happy smile. Maybe he was just proud of his own choice—or was there something more?

They walked together to the ball. Despite its appearance, the suit was not hot. In fact, it kept him cool and didn't prickle or bother him in any way. If anything, he should be feeling comfortable, if it weren't for the fact he was wearing bright red.

They walked through long corridors he had never seen and eventually came to a huge hall with white marble walls and columns. Sian whispered, "Whatever happens, don't do anything stupid." What a pointless thing to say. What can one do at a ball?

There were many people there, all well-dressed. The women wore impressive puffy dresses. He looked around to see if he found Cayla in one of them, but didn't see her. On a platform in the corner, sat the King and his entourage. It was the first time Darian saw him in person. He looked much younger than Darian had expected. His face was warm and friendly. How deceiving. He sat on a throne beside a beautiful blond woman—his wife. Nobody was allowed to say she was the queen, because the King was the only king. A tall, bald man stood beside him—the king's counselor. On the king's other side there were two smaller thrones where his two daughters sat. The younger princess wore a puffy blue dress. The older princess wore a shiny white dress that didn't shine as much as her black hair.

Darian stopped. The princess looked sideways and he couldn't see her face. *That hair.* But it couldn't be... The princess turned and looked at him. A smile of recognition lit her face. She was happy to see him.

The world stopped while Darian tried to catch his breath. The princess was gorgeous, but it was uncanny, as if she were Cayla's strange doppelganger, not the girl he considered his friend. She wore large earrings and a choker necklace with a white stone. While they looked beautiful on her, they just didn't fit with his idea of Cayla. And what was she doing sitting there by the evil king?

Darian stopped and remembered: royal quarters, her surprise when he didn't recognize her, the secret garden... It should have been obvious, if only he could have accepted that the mysterious girl who reminded him of home was not someone normal like him. But why wouldn't she tell him? He looked away, feeling betrayed. The beautiful girl sitting by the king looked like a girly girl, not someone who would climb trees and fight like a boy. Now, Darian had no problem with girly girls, but that wasn't Cayla.

Darian didn't make eye contact again, but from the corner of his eye, he noticed the way she followed his movements. He walked with his brother to a table near General Keen. Sian was probably having the chuckle of his life, but didn't show it. He introduced Darian to some high-ranking people from the army. There were also some rich merchants and the prince and attendants from Arlenia. Darian sat, thinking the bright red was perfect. He looked the way he felt—like a fool.

A band started playing. They had instruments Darian had never seen before that played music different from the music he had grown up with in his village. Men and women went to the center of the room, held hands and moved in little steps to one side and then the other. That was supposed to be dancing, even though it looked nothing like it. Darian thought it was boring.

He avoided looking at Cayla, but he glanced sometimes. She sat on her small throne. A young man, the prince of Arlenia, approached her. She smiled, and they got up. Cayla glanced at Darian before going to the middle of the hall with the young prince. They were dancing. He was holding her hands. *Her hands.* Darian hated that ball.

Sian sat beside him and whispered, "You can also ask her to dance, you know? It's allowed."

"I don't know how to dance."

"So don't glare at them, brother, it's getting obvious."

Sian laughed and got up to mingle. He moved among groups of older men, younger men, and women. Some girls pointed at Darian. Meanwhile, a couple girls approached Darian and asked him to dance. He refused politely, explaining he didn't know how to dance.

When Sian came back he said, "You are indeed dashing, little brother. All the girls are asking who you are."

"And what did you tell them?"

"I'm telling them you're my grumpy little brother and they should have me instead."

"Don't they get angry?"

"Some do. Some think it's a good idea." He laughed. "Then I have to explain I don't want to offend any of them by choosing only one and they all get angry in the end."

Darian rolled his eyes. He looked around and saw Cayla dancing. It was her fourth dance. At least each had been with a different man. She had stopped glancing at Darian and now just ignored him.

Sian glanced in her direction, then back at his brother. "You know, if you don't go talk to her, she won't come talk to you."

Darian shrugged. "What's the difference? If she's not supposed to be seen with me, maybe it's better that way."

"She's not supposed to be seen alone with you. This is a ball. Everyone talks to everyone. It's different."

"She's obviously too busy to pay attention to me."

"Well, if you don't pay attention to her, she'll sure be too busy, little brother."

Sian got up. Darian felt relieved. He wasn't sure if his brother meant to help him or was just trying to annoy him. As for Darian's clothes, there were indeed many eyes on him, but he wondered whether that was the good kind of attention. Anyways, the attention everyone was giving Cayla didn't make him feel good at all.

What was it that bothered him so much about seeing Cayla in a pretty dress, dancing with handsome young men, even a prince from another kingdom? Was it seeing other eyes on her? Seeing them touching her hands? Her hands. Even Darian had never held her hands like that.

Ugh. Darian wasn't jealous. He shouldn't be jealous. He knew it was wrong. Cayla was free to dance with whoever she wanted, to talk with any and all handsome young men, and to smile at whoever she wished. If she liked him, it wouldn't make a difference. If Darian only knew that she liked him.

Up until a few days before, Cayla lived in a little world only the two of them inhabited. He didn't need to worry about what she looked like or if anyone else thought she was lovely. Lovely. She was. But would they know her for the fierce, free girl who liked to climb trees and wrestle? Or would they expect her to be the odd well-mannered, well-dressed doppelganger—the beautiful girl with dark hair who looked like Cayla, who glanced at him like Cayla, but who couldn't be her. Perhaps it was just that Darian realized he had competition and wasn't sure if he was up to the challenge. Those were young men. Men. In comparison to Cayla's dance partners, Darian was a scrawny boy. But she was just a girl. His friend.

Darian looked around. Sian was talking to a group of girls. He gesticulated and laughed, and the girls laughed as well. He seemed happy and at ease at the ball, but he hadn't danced with anyone yet. The music stopped. Darian looked for Cayla, but she was neither on her throne or the dance floor. He looked around to see if she was among any of the groups, talking, but he didn't see her. He began to fear she had gone outside with someone when a girl cleared her throat beside him.

It was Cayla, standing next to him. "Are you going to ignore me all night?"

"I wasn't sure how to approach your majesty."

Cayla sat beside him. "It's me, Darian. What's wrong with you?"

"Were you going to tell me? Or was this some kind of joke?"

She seemed surprised and hurt. "What?"

He glanced at the throne. "The kind of work your father does in the castle."

She looked down. "I thought you knew. I asked if you knew who I am. You said you did. Are you going to be upset now?"

He crossed his arms. "I'm not upset."

She smiled. "We could dance then."

"I don't know these dances and I don't like dancing."

"I don't like dancing either," she said.

"Oh, you looked like you were having a lot of fun."

She laughed. "Are you jealous?" She then became serious. "You know we're just friends, right? You never..." She lowered her head.

Her words stung. "No pretension here. I just noticed you were enjoying yourself."

"I was being polite, that's all. Do you want to dance? I can teach you. That way we can talk longer." She looked at him. "Please."

It was hard to say no when she asked him like that. He got up and walked with her to the center of the hall. He held her hands and squeezed them. She squeezed them back, sending a wave of energy from his hands to his entire body.

She stared at him. "You know, you look ridiculous."

He stared back at her. "At least I don't have beetles hanging from my ears."

She laughed. "I know. You don't have to say it. At least we're even."

"You prefer me in my nightclothes?"

"Actually, I like it when you open your door shirtless."

He remembered that. What a blunder. His face got hot.

"There," she said. "Now you match your outfit."

"That was so impolite. I'm sorry."

She whispered, "I really liked it." There was something teasing and challenging in the way she looked at him.

He wasn't sure how to reply. When she looked down as if embarrassed, he said, "I was joking about the beetles. You look beautiful."

She smiled. "You look good too. Just… quite… eye-catching." She laughed. "But you're sounding like everyone else."

He was confused. "What?"

She rolled her eyes. "You look beautiful. That's what everyone says."

"Who says that?"

She laughed. "Everyone who dances with me. I'm sure they say it to all the girls. It's meaningless. Say something different."

Darian laughed. "Well, then, if you want to hear the truth, I prefer you when your hair is down and you wear a simple summer dress. In fact, I love it when you have dirt and grass in your hair."

She laughed. "Only you could say that."

"Why? You don't usually roll on the grass with other guys?"

"Nope. You see? They might get the boring dancing, but you get me on the ground."

His heart beat faster. "I hope we do more of that."

She smiled, then Darian felt her being pulled away. It was Sian. He said, "Sorry, older brothers get preference."

Cayla seemed puzzled. Sian kissed her hand, then started stepping sideways with her.

Darian was also puzzled, but he walked back to his seat. It was true that for a moment he had forgotten everything, forgotten where he was, forgotten that they were right in front of her father.

Sian danced with Cayla, then whispered something in her ear. She glanced at Darian, seeming annoyed, and tried to walk away. Sian held her and said something else. They kept dancing. She obviously hated it.

Darian looked at the throne. The bald king's counselor stared at Darian. There was something scary about the way he looked at him. The king's wife looked at him as well. They had noticed something. Oh, at least he was partly fulfilling his brother's wish and had a few eyes on him. When the music stopped, Cayla went back to her throne. She didn't look in Darian's direction. Sian walked around for a while, then sat beside Darian.

"What's wrong with you?" Darian asked. "Weren't you the one who suggested we dance?"

"Dance. Not stand in the middle of the floor staring at each other as if you wanted to do, you know, something more."

Darian was furious, but he spoke in a calm tone. "That's disrespectful."

"Not at all. If you both trust each other and if you're both into it—"

"She's fourteen."

"There's a huge difference between wanting and doing. I never said you wouldn't wait."

Sian was out to get on his nerves, but reacting would be worse. "What did you tell her?"

Sian shrugged. "What I just told you."

"You're disgusting. You can't have told her that."

"It was the truth."

"It isn't. While I admit I like her, I never thought about anything other than kissing her, and I'm sure… I'm not sure she even thought of that."

"I don't doubt you. Appearances can be deceiving."

To be fair, she did mention she liked to see him shirtless and they did say they wanted to roll on the grass. But Cayla was light, playful and innocent. It wasn't… He couldn't believe his brother had meddled like that.

"Great. Well, now you don't have to worry about my safety. She'll probably think I'm a pervert and won't talk to me."

Sian didn't seem bothered. "As long as her father doesn't think that, I don't really care."

Darian glanced at Cayla sitting on her throne. He knew that coming to the ball had been a mistake.

"I care," Darian said. "She was my only friend here."

"I'm not expecting thanks or anything, but I just saved your life."

"Even if you did, you didn't have to tell her your opinion of what our interaction looked like."

"You didn't have to stand there and look so obvious. Somebody has to say the hard truths." He got up. "I'll leave you here sulking."

Darian got up as well. "I'm going to bed."

"No," Sian said. "We'll stay here until our father says we can go."

Darian sat back. Cayla stepped on the dance floor again with another young man. She glanced in Darian's direction. She didn't seem angry at him. She was probably just furious with Sian, but he didn't blame her.

Suddenly, Darian didn't feel bothered by seeing her dancing with someone else. She was right. Maybe they saw beautiful, well-dressed Cayla, who gave them polite smiles. Free, wild Cayla was Darian's only. He glanced again at her and she glanced back. It didn't matter if he was sitting and she was standing. It didn't matter who was holding her hand. He saw her face looking at him and his heart warmed. He liked her. He did. And he didn't care who her father was.

6

SIAN

Darian had been called to a meeting with his father. That was all they had: meetings, official dinners, no normal interactions. In a way, it was better; Darian still wasn't sure how he felt about Keen's command of the army and still felt somewhat ashamed of being in the castle so close to the king. He knew of some of the things he had ordered and knew his mother had fought him. Darian's only consolation was knowing there were still some good people in the army and the faint hope that he could make a bigger difference closer to the center of power. He just hadn't figured out how yet.

Still, Darian saw his father when he was asked—or ordered. He was never given a choice. He now understood why Leena had told him he would not have the option of returning home once he met him. So there he was. And again Darian wondered if it was not just a way to excuse himself for living in the castle and receiving his father's favors. But what did it matter now?

He walked into the room of the meeting. Sian and Keen were already there.

Sian rolled his eyes. "Late, brother."

"I'm right on time. If you wanted me to come early, you could have told me." Shivers went down Darian's spine as he remembered his mother.

He sat in an armchair by his brother, facing his father.

"My sons," Keen said. "I can't tell you how happy I am to have our family reunited at last."

From the corner of his eye, Darian saw his brother grimace and glance at him.

Keen continued, "It has always been my desire to see one of you as the king of this land."

Darian was stunned. King? Wasn't his father already serving the king?

Keen said, "If not king, at least in a high command position in the army. For that reason, I want to make sure you two start as early as possible. I'm going to split the army command of the kingdom. Darian will take the South, Sian the North."

Sian said, "My brother hasn't done even half of the training. He has no experience whatsoever."

Keen waved his hand dismissively. "He'll learn by doing. He'll be well guided. What I want to make sure is that our family has control over this kingdom."

Darian didn't like what he heard, but on the other hand, it could be his chance to make a difference.

Sian asked, "What about Siphoria?"

"What about it?"

"Two years ago you asked me to take care of the crime in the city. I think I've been doing a great job."

Keen nodded. "You have, my son, you have." He had a malicious smile. "I know what you like in that city. But wars are not won by controlling criminals."

Sian sat back, eyebrows raised.

Keen continued, "If it makes you happy, your part will still include Siphoria. I just think you can do more. Think that you could take care of the crime in half of the Kingdom. Wouldn't you like that?" He looked at both Darian and Sian. "You will succeed me. You need to be ready."

Darian said, "I grew up in the North, I just think I—"

"You won't be able to do what's necessary," Keen said. "You'll need to think like a leader, not like a poor villager."

I wasn't poor, Darian thought, but he kept it to himself.

Sian said, "Darian can't even control a lift. He can't—"

"He'll learn," Keen said. "Get him out of the initial training. I wanted him to do it just to toughen up. Become a man." He pointed to Sian. "Like you did. Now he can learn to be a leader. And a pilot." He stared at both boys. "I trust you to make sure our family remains in power. As long as we have control over the army, we have control over Whyland."

Sian sighed. "And when are we supposed to take our new positions?"

"Once Darian is ready. I imagine a month or so from now."

"Will we have to move?" Sian asked.

"You'll have to travel, but you can keep living here—Sian in the academy, Darian in the castle."

Darian asked, "Why the difference?"

Keen leaned forward and looked at Darian. "I'm making up for a life without you, my son."

His brother made a loud breathing noise. Darian understood it was a little unfair. Maybe he should ask to live in the military academy with his brother, but he wanted to remain in the castle because of Cayla, so he asked, "Can't Sian live here as well?"

Keen winked. "Your brother likes the city."

Sian shrugged and looked away. "True."

Keen smiled. "That's my son. Sian, make sure your brother's prepared."

"I will, father," Sian replied.

"Very well. You are both dismissed."

As Darian walked out, Sian said, "I want to talk to you. In private."

They both went to Darian's bedroom. Sian looked around. "This is huge. You sure are treated like a prince."

"You could live here as well, couldn't you?"

Sian gave him a half smile. "Could I? I'm not sure you noticed, but I wasn't given a choice."

"But you like Siphoria."

"I was raised in the military academy. Siphoria was the only place where I could feel like a human being, a person."

Darian looked down. "I'm sorry."

"Save your sorry and your empty words. You have no idea, no idea what it's been like." Sian leaned against a wall, closed his eyes and laughed, then looked at Darian. "I'm almost sixteen. Do you want to know when I started to train? When I moved to the academy?"

"I assume eleven or twelve…"

"Five. But my father came by—oh he did—to make sure I was being properly trained." Sian chuckled. "He wanted to make sure I developed character, that I became a man. I had to learn to endure hunger, to endure pain. I did." He burst into laughter. "So useful."

Darian was shocked. He wanted to say something, but wasn't sure what. "It must have been hard."

"No kidding. I'll tell you more. As I was growing up, my father told me I deserved nothing and wouldn't be his son if I didn't show him how strong I was. I had to earn his love. No, scrap that. Love is poison, he says. It kills you slowly. I had to earn his respect." Sian's voice started cracking. "And then you come by. Oh, no, you don't need any of that. Oh, you'll live in the castle and have all the luxury I never had. And finally, without any training, any effort, you'll get to control half the army. Isn't that wonderful?"

Darian looked down. "I could talk to him. I could ask him to give you a larger portion. I don't know."

Sian shook his head. "It doesn't change anything, mommy's little boy. You're pretty like your mommy and you'll get everything handed down on a tray for you."

"You have Siphoria, don't you? You said you took care of the crime there. You should be proud."

"Oh, I've got tons of pride. I'm a shell of it in case you haven't noticed. And yet, I've ruined my reputation. People think I'm some kind of degenerate."

"I don't think that. I still admire you for what you did at the prison."

"You think I was being noble? I wasn't. I was looking for some friends."

Darian looked at his brother, so hurt, so vulnerable, and wished he could do something. Then an image came to his mind. And a voice. His mother's.

My son, my son, my sons. Tell him I love him.

Of course! That was why Darian had to find his father—for his brother.

"Sian, there's something I need to tell you. Our mother, as she was dying, she asked me to tell you she'd always loved you. She asked me to find you."

Sian stopped leaning on the wall and stood. "She said that? Well, doesn't that make everything all right?" Sarcasm and bitterness were clear in his voice.

"I don't mean—"

Sian stared at Darian. "I was two. I still remember it. I know I shouldn't remember, but I do. She ran with you. I yelled. I yelled as much as a child can yell." Darian saw in his brother the eyes of the little sad boy within him. Sian snorted. "She never heard me. She never turned back. I was with our father. She'd run away. I was told you two died shortly after that. A few months ago I learned it wasn't true. Not that she ever bothered asking where I was."

"She was running from our father. I know she was. Our entire village was. Maybe she couldn't—"

"I'm not blaming her. I'm pretty sure I wasn't worth the trouble."

"Don't say that."

"It's true. I don't care. She's not my mother."

Darian looked down. He felt sad, sorry, but he didn't know what he could do. "How can I make up for that?"

"For starters, you could stop existing. How's that?"

Darian just stared.

Sian said, "Fine, you can't do that. Just leave me alone. Don't ever mention your mother."

"I wasn't the one who—"

Sian shook his head. "Whatever. Forget what you just heard. It was a moment of insanity." He shrugged then smiled. "These things don't bother me." He turned around to leave.

"Wait," Darian said. "Didn't you have something to tell me? Is it about our father?"

Sian shrugged. "I lost my thought. We'll catch up later."

He left.

Darian stared at the closed door, the wall his brother had leaned against, and felt empty and powerless. He wished he could mend the distance between them, but had no idea how. If he already disliked his father, now he did even more. As for his mother, Darian thought she had done what she had to do to hide and protect him. She must have tried to save Sian as well, but wasn't able to. It wasn't as if she could just knock on General Keen's door and ask for him to give her son back. The general would likely have tracked her and taken Darian as well. She had chosen to sacrifice one son in order to keep the other. The realization didn't hurt any less. And it sure didn't hurt any less for Sian.

. . .

Darian didn't go to the academy the next day. He was taken to a lift field instead. Lifts were the flying machines Darian had learned to fear, and later respect, in his village. Darian was going to learn how to pilot them. In a way he was happy; he would get a more important position and be one step closer to being able to make a difference for good. Or so he hoped.

7

WRESTLING WITH FEELINGS

Darian had dinner with his father, then went to his room. He was going to read and study. Three knocks on the door startled him. He thought it might be Cayla, but he didn't want to get his hopes up. Maybe it was his brother, but Sian didn't knock like that.

Darian opened the door and his heart raced. Cayla stood there, hair loose, wearing a summer dress and sandals.

"Do you want to go for a walk?" she asked.

"Sure."

He followed her. She walked in a different direction this time. They descended stairs and came to a door to a different garden. It didn't have trees but beautiful flowers. It was also encircled by high walls.

She asked, "It was your brother, wasn't it? Who sent me the message not to see you anymore?"

"It was. But I think he was just trying to protect me."

She chuckled. "You believe that? He's a prick and he's obviously jealous of you."

"Leave my brother. One thing doesn't have anything to do with the other."

"I hope one brother doesn't have anything to do with the other. You're not like him, are you?"

"I don't know him well." There was a question he had to ask. "But is he right? Will your father get angry if he sees you with me?"

"These are our private gardens. I'm allowed to come here as much as I want."

Allowed. There was something unpleasant about that. "Do you usually bring a friend with you?"

She squinted and stared at him. "What do you think?"

He shrugged. "You could come with your sister, a friend, I don't know."

"Oh, that. No. I'm the lonely type. And I never had a friend like you, if that's what you're asking."

What kind of friend? He held the question, and said, "I don't want you to get in trouble."

She looked straight at him with challenging eyes. "I don't care. Now you—is it that you don't want me to get in trouble or are you afraid? If you're afraid, you can go."

"I'm not afraid."

She smiled. "Good." She pointed to a flowerless patch of grass. "I've been dying to practice more wrestling."

That was what she wanted? Darian hid his disappointment as well as he could. After the ball, after what she'd told him, after the way she'd looked at him, he had expected something different. But that wasn't even the problem. Since he started to think about her, well, in that way, he didn't think he would be able to grab her and go to the ground without thinking stuff he shouldn't be thinking. And there he was thinking right now. He closed his eyes and took a deep breath. "Cayla, I know you're good at it and you want to get better, but I don't think you should—"

"It's that now? Why? Because now you know I'm the princess? You're going to treat me like some kind of fragile flower? I thought you were different."

"You're not a fragile flower and I'm not treating you like one."

"Then what is it? I'm not good enough for you to practice with?"

"You are, but… Anyways, I'm done with the fighting. I'm learning to pilot now."

"Great. Who cares if she wants to learn self-defense? Who cares what she thinks? I'm done with it and I don't care."

"What about you? You want a practice buddy, find a practice buddy. Don't pretend to…" He stopped.

"To what?"

"To be my friend."

"Friends do things together."

Darian swallowed. He hoped she had no idea of the things he wished they did together. "We can talk."

"We can find a middle ground—how's that? We practice a little, then do whatever you want. You were helping me. It's not fair."

"It's not that. I swear. It's just that you are a girl and I'm a guy, and… I don't want to, uh, be touching you. It could be inappropriate."

She sighed and said, "Darian, it's me and you. Nothing's inappropriate."

Her tone was sweeter than ever, but she must have had no idea what he'd been thinking. In a way, he felt bad, as if he were crossing a mental line he shouldn't cross, but on the other hand, she was the one who'd started. *I like to see you shirtless.* Well, what did she expect? He took a deep breath and shoved away those thoughts.

Cayla asked, "What's wrong?"

Darian decided to ask as much as he could. "You don't see anything wrong in me touching you?"

She rolled her eyes. "Why would I?" She looked down and seemed hurt. "You're being weird." She shook her hands in front of her. "Fine then. Don't touch me. What a horrible thing that would be." She sounded angry. She turned around and started walking away.

He rushed towards her and put a hand on her shoulder. "Hey, hey, not that. Stay. I was just trying to be respectful. That was all."

She turned and looked at him. "Why did you change?"

"I didn't. I just missed you. It's just…" He stopped, unsure of what to say.

"It's what?"

He closed his eyes. He wasn't sure how she saw him. Did she see him as a friend only? A practice buddy? Maybe she didn't even realize he was a boy. Maybe that was why she thought he was so different from other guys. Maybe she didn't expect him to think about her that way. But then, sometimes he thought she liked him the same way he liked her, and that she liked to tease him. Either way, he didn't want to upset her.

"You know what? I was being silly. I learned a lot with you and I respect you as an adversary. Of course we can practice."

She smiled. "Phew. I was starting to think you were bitten by a bug or something. You'd start to say: my dear princess Cayla, even the stars envy your beauty."

That annoyed him. "Who said that?"

She shrugged. "I told you everyone says stuff like that. Not necessarily that, but just as idiotic."

He still felt hurt. "And I can't think you're pretty?"

"*You* can." That emphasis. Wow, that emphasis. "You'd never say anything idiotic or make it the center of our conversation."

He laughed. "Well, your hair is like the night sky, your eyes like the stars, and your smile is a half-moon illuminating the night. Like it?"

She burst out laughing. "Charming. I'm going to fall in love just because you noticed my hair is black."

"You should. I'm so poetic."

She shook her head and then looked away. "I'd only fall in love with someone who respects me as an equal, not a pretty prize." She glanced at him.

He caught his breath. He wasn't sure if she meant she could fall in love with him, if she'd fallen in love already, or if she was explaining what it would take for her to fall in love. Regardless, the hint was clear.

He walked to the path of grass she'd pointed out. "How do you want to start?"

She followed him and smiled. "Now you're interested. What a change."

"I told you, I was being stupid."

"Are you going to touch me like a flower?"

He decided to be straightforward. "I'll touch you however you want."

She laughed.

"What?" He asked.

"You sound funny."

Great. Maybe she did see him as only her stupid practice buddy. "You're going to mock me now?"

"No. Not that. It's just… You sounded like…" She looked down.

"I'm talking about wrestling, in case it wasn't clear. Cause that's all you care about, right?"

She squinted. "Still on that?"

He shook his head. "I'm just saying it's something important to you. I still think you should learn different combat techniques."

"But I do. Odell teaches me."

His heart beat faster. "Who's Odell?"

She rolled her eyes. "My father's counselor. He's my teacher. He's old and he's ugly. You aren't jealous, are you?"

He shrugged. "Why would I be?"

She looked away. "No reason."

"If you know the answer you don't have to ask."

"I didn't know it was obvious." Cayla squinted. "Thanks for clarifying."

She seemed mad, but this game of push and pull had left *him* confused. It was better to focus on practicing. "How do you want to start? Any special move?"

"No. I think I've got it. I doubt you can throw me on the ground."

"You're daring me?"

She smiled. "Maybe. Maybe that's why you don't want to practice. You don't want to lose to a girl."

"There's nothing to that. You're strong and you're good."

"Well, I'm sick of you taking it easy on me. I want to beat you fair and square." She was definitely in a mood to tease and test him.

"As you wish, princess."

"My title is not an offense."

"I meant none."

She tilted her head. "I'm waiting. Take me down."

Darian advanced. He knew she was going to try to trip him with her right leg. Maybe he had been taking it easy on her—he could predict her moves. He jumped to his right and tried to trip her left leg, but she had predicted that as well. She stood sideways and pushed him. He grabbed her left arm and pulled her beneath him. He was lying on top of her, pinning her arms. "Like this?"

She smiled. "Impressive."

"Do you want a rematch?"

She smiled. "No hurry."

No hurry. Cayla was nuts. First she'd been teasing him to wrestle her and now she seemed happy where she was.

Where she was. Their positions dawned on him and he felt her body beneath him. Her eyes met his in surprise, then relaxed, opening wide—a lake his own eyes dove into. He loosened his grip on her wrists and slid his hands from her arms to her waist. She put her arms around him.

He'd never been so close to a girl before, but he didn't feel awkward or afraid. It felt right, natural. It felt good to feel her close to him, to see her looking at him like that. He wanted to relish each moment.

She touched his face and he turned and started to kiss her wrist. She closed her eyes and smiled. He then kissed her cheek and kept kissing, slowly making his way to her lips. He'd been dreaming of kissing her for a while now, but he'd never imagined it would be like this or that they would be so close. She liked him. Him. His lips reached the corner of her mouth. She turned her head and their lips met.

The kiss never came.

Darian heard a loud boom. He raised his head to see what had caused it and saw five soldiers jumping down from the walls, guns pointed at them.

"Arrest him!" a man said. It was one of the high-ranking commanders Darian had seen at the ball. By his side, looking away, a person Darian could not believe was there: Sian.

Two soldiers grabbed Darian, while two others held Cayla.

Darian shouted, "Don't touch her!"

Sian whispered in his ear, "Be silent or it will be worse."

"I won't," Darian said.

His brother put a cloth with a strong smell in front of his nose and everything went dark. The last image in Darian's mind was Cayla, looking at him, fearful and worried.

DARIAN WOKE UP IN A CELL. He was sitting on a chair and his hands and feet were in shackles. He heard a voice say, "He woke up."

The door to his cell opened, and he saw that army commander and Sian by his side.

The commander said, "You're under severe accusations, boy. You're lucky your brother cares for you. He wants you to have a clean, painless death."

Sian looked away, his face a mask.

"What accusations?" Darian asked.

The commander laughed. "If you don't know what you did, I'm not going to tell you."

Darian hated to ask this question, but he had to: "Where's my father?"

The commander laughed. "Your father? He disowned you and won't be involved."

"What about Cayla?"

Sian shook his head. But what did Darian care?

The commander said, "She claims you were assaulting her, the king's daughter. The penalty is death. We'll see about the clean death later."

The commander and Sian left. Darian had a hard time believing Cayla would accuse him, but then, he had no idea what she was going through, and if she had to make up lies to save herself. Who knows, they could have tortured her. The thought filled him with dread.

It was hard to believe his life would end like this and that he would never do anything meaningful. But then, his life had been nothing but emptiness since his mother had died. The one bright spot had been Cayla. He'd die thinking about the moment they had looked into each other's eyes. His only regret was that they had never kissed.

And Sian—how could he have betrayed him like this? All this time, pretending to help him when in fact he wanted to catch him. He hoped his death would make his brother happy.

It was hard to sleep when he could not lie down, but he eventually dozed off. He had the impression that he saw his brother in the middle of the night, but he wasn't sure. At some point, someone shook his shoulder.

Darian opened his eyes and saw a bald man in a long robe. It took him some time to realize it was the king's counselor. He had keys and opened Darian's shackles. The door of the cell was open.

The man said, "I'm Odell and I come as a friend. I'm here to help you."

"You also want to give me a clean death?"

"I said I come as a friend. I'm Cayla's teacher. She's almost like a daughter to me, so you'll understand my concern."

"How is she?"

"She threatened to kill herself."

"No."

"Her father told her to go ahead. I think she was bluffing, but I told her I'd help you."

"Don't let anything happen to her." He looked down. "I didn't do anything. We didn't do anything."

"I know."

"Tell the king, then!"

"It's not that simple— we'll have to be diplomatic—but first there's something I want from you."

"What?"

"The truth—if you're willing to give it to me. I want to make sure I can trust you."

Darian shrugged. "You can ask anything you want—"

"It's… more complicated than that. I have a potion. It will make you tell the truth."

"Aren't potions forbidden?"

"Sometimes we need extreme measures."

"And you want me to drink it, so you can question me?"

"Yes."

Darian shrugged. "I have nothing to hide."

"You're quite confident! But see, I must warn you: this potion can be quite unsettling. You may say things even you weren't aware of. And there's more: you must not fight it or it could suffocate and kill you."

This sounded dangerous. "And what do I get if I drink it and answer your questions?"

"You don't have to drink it. I'll save your life anyway. I just want to know if I should make her forget you."

"I'll drink it." Darian looked around. The cell door was open and the hall was silent. "Where's everybody?"

"I made them sleep for a while. We'll need privacy." He invited Darian to a table in a corner. He hadn't seen it because it was behind his chair. There was water and bread. Odell said, "Eat and drink, but not too much, or you might feel sick."

Darian drank some water and ate some pieces of bread.

He was starving, but he wanted to do this potion thing and maybe find a way to survive. Odell was strange but he seemed concerned about Cayla, and it was true she'd mentioned that he was teaching her to fight. Plus, Darian knew he'd done nothing wrong and was eager at having a chance to prove his innocence.

Odell took a flask and handed it to Darian. The man said, "Drink slowly and relax. Don't fight it."

The drink was thick and viscous. It wasn't even liquid, it was more like a paste, and tasted horrible.

"You can drink some water," Odell said.

Darian drank, to help him swallow. What was that thing?

"How do you feel?" Odell asked.

"Afraid," Darian said. He'd meant to say he felt normal.

"Good, good," Odell said. "Now, I'm going to start asking questions. Just relax and say whatever comes to mind. Don't try to control or fight what you're saying. You will say things you might think are lies. Don't fight it. You will answer my questions and say nothing else. I'm bringing out the truth within you. The truth is coming out." He snapped his fingers. "What's your name?"

"Darian."

"And your full name?"

"We don't use them where I come from."

"Where were you born?"

That was easy—his village—but he said something else. "I don't know."

"How come?"

"My mother was on the run and I'm not sure if the story

she told me about my childhood is true." Darian felt as if there was a stranger within him answering the questions.

Odell nodded. "How long have you known Cayla?"

The stranger within him didn't say anything odd this time. "Since my first night at the castle. Five months ago."

"How did you meet her?"

"I felt something calling me. I left my room and then stumbled on her." What?

"Did you know she was the princess?"

"Yes and no." Bizarre answer.

Odell raised his eyebrows. "How come?"

"I knew she was the princess, but I convinced myself she wasn't." Another bizarre answer.

"Why?"

"I didn't want to believe that anything existed outside our garden, outside me and her."

"I understand you went with her to the private gardens. What did you do during those times?"

"She climbed trees, we talked, sometimes we practiced wrestling."

"Why would you wrestle with her?"

"Because she asked." The answers were getting better.

"Were you interested in learning to fight or in grabbing her?"

"Neither."

"What were you interested in?"

"Seeing her smile." The potion stranger inside him was doing a much better job.

"What do you think of the fact she's the princess?"

"Her father's a tyrant who won't last on the throne much

longer." What? What had he just said? Darian felt he had just signed his death sentence. He wanted to protest, but his body was limp and he couldn't talk. He decided to relax and let the words come. Considering he'd already been sentenced to death, nothing worse could happen to him.

"Do you think she's in love with you?"

"I'm positive." That was quite a confident potion stranger.

"Since when?"

"It was gradual, from the night she met me." What?

"Were you taking advantage of the fact she was in love with you?"

"No."

"Why?"

"I was too dumb to notice it."

Odell laughed. "When and how did you notice it?"

"At the ball. She stared at me the whole night. She squeezed my hand. She told me…" Darian's throat closed. He endured the pain. He wasn't going to tell him what she'd said.

Odell snapped his fingers. "Question answered. That's fine." Darian's throat opened and he could breathe. Odell then asked, "What do you think about your father?"

"He's a sadistic maniac who damaged my brother."

"What do you think about your brother?"

Darian didn't understand why he was being asked that, but it obviously didn't matter because his mouth started speaking. "He's hurt and broken."

"What were you doing last night when the guards came?"

"I was lying on top of Cayla, kissing her cheek."

"What were you thinking?"

"I wasn't thinking."

"How did you come to that position?"

"Wrestling."

Odell rolled his eyes. "Of course. And did you suggest wrestling so you could get close to her?"

"I didn't suggest it."

"She did?"

"Yes."

"Are you interested in her money?"

"Soon she won't have any." Death sentence.

"Are you interested in her claim to the throne?"

"Soon she won't have any claim."

"Why do you think she likes you?"

"She's smart and has good taste." Conceited potion stranger.

"And do you like her?"

"I'm in love with her."

"Why?"

"I feel good around her. Happy."

Odell smiled. "Very well." He snapped his fingers. "Truth out."

Darian was himself again and could speak. "It wasn't me. I would never say those things, I —"

"I told you it was unsettling."

"I'm not a traitor to the king."

"I'll ignore that. You must be angry because he imprisoned you, that's all. I'll never mention anything you said to anyone. Now, I will make sure you are freed. There will be an audience tomorrow. Whatever happens, you must say you are her friend and only her friend. Never mention the kissing. Never mention you are in love. Pretend you don't care about her if it comes to it. I'll tell her to do the same. You might see her, and it might hurt, but don't show your feelings.

"Also, as much as I hate your father, he didn't disown you. He'll try to get you transferred, but he can't defend you openly. Your brother is part of the accusation committee. I don't know what he's planning. I don't know if he's there to protect you or to gain favors. Don't trust him."

"I don't." That hurt, but it was true.

"Well, then, tomorrow you'll have a long day. Don't tell anyone I've been here."

"You had it all planned. Why did you make me drink that thing?"

"Word was out you were taking advantage of Cayla. I wanted to make sure it wasn't true. But you answered the questions well. You truly like her. It might be a silly teenage crush, but you think it's true love. You're just kids being kids."

He pulled the chains and pointed to the chair in the middle of the cell. "I'll have to put you back in your shackles or the guards will be spooked. Be confident. Tomorrow you'll find your freedom."

"After tomorrow, I won't see her again, will I?"

"No. But trust me, it will pass. Soon you'll forget her."

"You'll also make sure she forgets me?"

"I'll do what I can to make sure she's happy." He smiled.

"But you're a nice boy and maybe one day you could make her happy. It just won't be anytime soon."

Darian had one last question. "Is it true that she's been accusing me of—" He couldn't finish the sentence.

Odell shook his head. "Not true. Lalus wants to pit you against each other. He also told her you said horrible things about her."

So Lalus was the commander's name. "Did she believe him?"

"I don't know. She showed no reaction. I have to go now. Try to rest." He looked at Darian's uncomfortable position. "As well as you can."

Darian sighed. He was more hopeful now. If he could survive, if he could escape, he could dream again, he could make plans.

And one day, he could return.

8

THE AUDIENCE

"Wake up, sleepy!" Sian's voice echoed in the cell.

Darian opened his eyes. His brother had a key and opened his shackles. He had three guards with him and a satisfied smile on his face.

"Why did you do it?" Darian asked.

"My loyalty is to the king and his family. But you should be happy. You have an audience."

Darian's body hurt from sleeping chained to the chair and he had difficulty getting up. Sian came to his side to help him, but Darian pushed him away. He took a step on his own, lost his balance and fell.

Sian lifted him to his feet. "Don't worry. A little stretching and you'll be back to normal. I guarantee it. But you'll need help for now."

Darian hated what his brother had done and hated having to lean on him, but didn't push him away. He let Sian guide him to a large circular hall. Chairs and stands surrounded an open area in the middle. The king, Odell, Lalus, and four soldiers were there. Darian was both disappointed and relieved that Cayla was not.

Odell cleared his throat. "This young man is accused of seeing the princess in secret. What do you have to say?"

Darian was glad he had to answer to Odell and not the king, and that he hadn't drunk any potion this time. He lowered his head. "I was just obeying the royal family. She ordered me and I obeyed. I thought it was my duty."

The king laughed. "My daughter claims she played with you like a puppy. My concern is: how much did you play?"

"I only did as she asked, your Highness."

"And did she ask you to lie on top of her?" This wasn't going well.

"I've never done what your highness is describing." Darian hated to act so humble.

Sian stepped up and kneeled in front of the king. "Your highness, if I may make a suggestion." His voice was calm, soothing almost. "The four soldiers who were present last night, as well as myself and Lalus, are here. Each soldier has spent the night in a separate cell without communication with me, Lalus, or each other. Now, if we are questioned as a group, we will say the same thing. If we are questioned alone, you'll know who is lying and who isn't. Therefore I ask that each of us be questioned separately." There was something oddly hypnotic about Sian's voice.

"That seems hardly necessary," Odell said, dissipating the effect of Sian's words. "We know what the accusations are."

He turned to the king. "They may have planned this before-hand. It sounds like a conspiracy to me."

The king stroked his beard. "Maybe. But I'm interested in what they have to say."

Odell called six guards. Each one accompanied one of the witnesses—Lalus, Sian, and the four soldiers.

Lalus came in first.

"Why did you go to the garden that night?" Odell asked.

"I was patrolling the castle. An informant told me Darian and Cayla were at the flower garden. I gathered some soldiers. On our way, Sian asked to join us. When we arrived, I saw Darian and Cayla together. I wanted to arrest them right then and there, but Sian advised us to watch them and gather evidence. They seemed to be talking. Even-tually, the boy pinned your daughter to the ground. She yelled, and we came to her rescue."

"Who informed you of their whereabouts?" Odell asked.

"Her attendant; the maid who helps her and cleans her room."

"Very well. You're dismissed."

Darian wasn't sure how this audience could be a good idea.

The next person brought in was Sian. He seemed calm and relaxed, almost amused.

"Why did you go to the garden last night?" Odell asked.

"I had been following my brother."

"Why?"

"I feared he might be seeing the princess in secret."

"What made you think that?"

"The ball." Sian threw a hard glance at Darian. "He looked at her too much."

Odell asked. "So you're saying it was your idea? Why would you go against your family?"

"My duty is to your Majesty and his family, nobody else."

"Where does Lalus come into this?"

"He saw me going to the garden and said he wanted to come with me. I thought it would be a good idea to have an older, more experienced member of the army with me."

"And what did you see?"

"Darian and Cayla were indeed in the garden."

"What were they doing?"

"Talking."

"Were they touching each other?"

"No."

Sian was lying. Maybe he regretted what he had done, or understood they were going too far.

"Why then did you arrest him?"

"He was meeting the princess in secret. I did not think it was allowed."

"Are you aware of the accusations brought against your brother?"

"Yes. I accused him personally of secrecy. The matter should be investigated."

"And not other accusations?"

"I've heard whispers. As far as I know, some people misinterpreted what happened. I hope the liars will be dealt with. They are tarnishing the princess' honor."

"And you don't know who the liars are, do you?"

"I can investigate."

"That won't be necessary for now. Very well. Dismissed."

Odell called in the first of the four soldiers present the previous night. As much as Darian hated Sian, he didn't want his brother to be punished for trying to defend him, and feared the soldier would contradict him. But to Darian's surprise, the soldier's answers were identical to Sian's. He said Sian had been the one who planned it, Lalus had joined them, and Darian and Cayla had only been talking. The three other soldiers confirmed the same story.

Even Odell seemed surprised. As the last soldier was dismissed, he said, "Well then, it seems we had a great misunderstanding."

"Lies are lies," the king said. "My daughter has been wrongly slandered and the responsible will die. Call in the witnesses except Lalus."

Sian and the soldiers came in. Sian looked tense.

"The sentence for lies is death," the king said. He turned to Darian, "You. You will carry the sentence. I want you to kill Lalus."

Really? Darian was going to be forced to kill a person?

Sian stepped in and knelt in front of the king. "He's a child. I, as his older brother, request permission to take his place."

Again Sian was defending him. He made mistakes—he did—but he made up for them.

The king smiled. "That will be fun. But you are Keen's older boy. I've heard you are a great fighter. I'd love to see it. Let's make this a death by combat—see who kills the other first. Lalus is a dear member of the army. I am happy to give him a chance to defend himself."

Darian's heart beat faster. He didn't want anything to happen to his brother. On the other hand, it was true that Sian was an excellent fighter.

Sian asked, "May we use any weapons?"

The king laughed. "No, bare hands will be more fun."

Odell whispered something to the king. The king then said, "Gruesome! Indeed. Get them swords."

Darian had no idea how good his brother was with a sword or if he had even practiced with old weapons. But Sian had asked for a weapon, so he must have had a good reason.

Lalus was called in. He walked with a confident air and a satisfied smiled.

The king said, "Walk to the middle. You'll fight Sian."

Lalus looked around, confused. "What?" He stared at Sian. "You. You lied! You planned this!"

"Quiet!" the king yelled. "You will duel, and then we'll know the truth. You both have an equal chance. I'm fair."

Lalus looked down. His face had changed. He looked afraid. A guard brought two swords and gave one to Sian and one to Lalus. Darian didn't like what was happening. He wished he could step up and stop that madness, but the King had five guards behind him with fire weapons. Incapable of defending his brother, he felt powerless. In that moment Darian decided he would do whatever it took to bring the king down. Cayla would understand.

Sian and Lalus walked to the center of the room. Sian seemed calmer than Lalus. Darian trusted that his brother's skill in hand-to-hand combat would keep him alive and unharmed. And where was his father in all this?

Lalus and Sian started circling each other. Lalus attacked and Sian blocked the strike. Sian stepped sideways and dodged another attack, then another, and another. Lalus seemed to have the advantage, but Sian persistently blocked his every move. There was something strange about the way his brother moved, though. Sian was slow, rigid, almost clumsy. It didn't make sense. Darian had never seen his brother spar, but he had tried to wrestle him, and Darian could never predict what Sian would do with his feet. Ten, fifteen, twenty times he'd tried, he always lost. Couldn't Sian use the same kind of movements now? In fact, as he looked, Lalus had strong blows but moved slowly. Sian could easily have already dropped him to the ground. What was his brother doing? What was he thinking?

The worst then happened; Sian fell backward. Lalus brought down his sword, and Sian rolled away just in time. The king was ecstatic, enjoying every moment. Sian was back to his feet in a single movement, defending himself. Sometimes he tried to hit Lalus, but with very poor attacks. Maybe Sian was trying to tire his opponent. Maybe a sword duel had different rules. And then, maybe Sian just didn't know how to fight with a sword.

Sian then fell again, but this time didn't roll away fast enough, and was hit in the arm. Sian's sword flew away from his hand. Darian tasted something bitter. The only reason he didn't ask the fight to be stopped was because the king would probably have him killed as well.

Lalus advanced towards Sian and thrust his sword towards his chest. Sian jumped to the side and pushed Lalus' sword hand down, causing the old man to stumble forward.

Sian then kicked the sword out of his hand and caught it midair. In less than a second, Sian had cut Lalus' throat.

He fell to the ground.

Sian kneeled and closed his eyes, then glanced at Darian. There was fear and horror on his face.

DARIAN PACKED IN HIS BEDROOM, as he'd been ordered to leave the city. He had been forbidden to come near the castle, Siphoria, or the princess ever again, not even to say goodbye. At least he was alive. His father had him transferred to a battalion far south, in the city of Eves. He hadn't seen him or his brother after the sentence was decided.

Hard knocks startled him. Darian opened the door.

It was Odell. "Follow me. You have an audience."

"Again?"

Odell smiled and whispered. "Don't you want to say goodbye to a friend?"

Darian felt hopeful, then cautious. "Is this a trap? Or a test?"

"I think I tested you all I could, didn't I? But hurry. You'll have little time."

They walked to a corridor Darian had never seen before and descended narrow stairs. Odell touched a wall and opened a door that didn't seem to be there before. Darian suspected the old man had dealings with magic, which was ironic if he was the king's counselor. Still, he was different from the king, and Darian almost trusted him. Almost. The old man gestured for Darian to go inside. The room looked like an upside-down bowl with walls and a ceiling that came together in one piece. Light came from a small circle in the middle. Odell said, "Don't worry. This room is secret. You won't be heard."

Darian looked around. He heard Cayla's voice before he saw her. "I'm sorry. You can't imagine how sorry I am."

She sat on a chair, sobbing. Her eyes were puffy and red, with dark shadows. Darian approached her and touched her face. "It's not your fault. At all. You couldn't have known."

She looked at him. "Can you forgive me?"

"There's nothing to forgive."

He'd never thought he'd see her like this—weak, vulnerable, and yet, so beautiful.

She looked down. "I would never have forgiven myself if… But I didn't know. I didn't know this would happen. I didn't."

He touched her hair and kissed her forehead. "Everything is fine. I'm here. I'm alive."

"We'll never see each other again."

"Of course we will. I'll come back. I'm not going far. Things change. Times change. Who knows? Your father might change his mind or something else could happen. I'll come back."

She smiled. He wiped away her tears. She squinted and said, "You'd better not forget you said that."

Darian laughed. "There. That's more like you. I don't like to see you sad."

"My father threatened to kill you. Do you have any idea how I felt?"

"I can imagine. But it's over now. And I will come back for you."

Cayla smiled. That smile. Darian could live off that smile. A crazy idea came to his mind. He didn't care about his plans, his father, his brother, defeating the evil king or anything. He said, "Come with me. Let's run away together. You won't be locked in this castle anymore. We can hide with my people."

She looked at him—her eyes said yes—but then she looked down. "We wouldn't be happy. We'd have to live on the run. And you'd risk getting killed."

Darian exhaled. She was right. "I know. We can wait."

He hoped she wouldn't forget him, He hoped they would stay connected. He pulled one of the necklaces from under his shirt. "I know this is not as beautiful or precious as your jewelry—and you don't have to wear it—but I'd like you to have it. To remember me." He showed her the other one. "One of these used to be my mother's. I don't know which; they are twins."

Cayla took it and looked at the black stone. "Thank you. It's beautiful. Of course I'll wear it."

She put it around her neck and leaned forward while Darian closed it. When he looked at the stone again, it was a clear yellow. He gasped.

Cayla was surprised as well. "It changed color." She looked at Darian. "Yours too."

It was true. His stone had turned a clear yellow. More distant words from his mother came to him. *These are twin necklaces. For people who love each other, or they'll hide their beauty. You can use them to communicate. I'll give you mine when you're old enough. You'll know if she loves you.*

Cayla loved him. He knew it, and yet…

Cayla asked, "What is it? What does it mean?"

"It means we're connected. That's why they changed colors."

Cayla looked down and smiled. He couldn't get over it. She loved him. He leaned forward, pulled up her chin and kissed her. Her lips tasted salty from the tears.

After a second, she turned her head away. "Darian, please. We need to be friends and friends only. Your life depends on it."

He sighed. He understood she was still afraid, so he hugged her instead. She leaned her face on his chest. He squeezed her as tight as he could. He wished they could remain like this forever, that he'd never have to let her go.

Darian's shirt dampened from her tears. He heard a knock on the door and knew his time was up. He kissed the top of her head. "I have to go. The stone—we can use it to communicate with each other. You press it and think about me."

"I'll do it all the time then."

He laughed. "You can *think* about me all the time, but only press the stone when you're alone and nobody sees you."

She looked at it. "Is it magic?"

"It's old, forgotten knowledge."

She nodded and looked into his eyes. "I'll wait for you."

He kissed her forehead. "And I'll be back."

9

CAYLA'S RESOLUTIONS

Cayla hated balls and hated dancing. She hated pretty dresses and stupid earrings. She crossed her hands over her chest. Cleavage. She felt naked. She hated the prince of Arlenia. But here she was at a ball being given in his stupid name. And he'd been dancing with her.

She wanted to puke as she remembered his slimy hands on hers, while staring at her as if he were a starved dog and she a steak. Arlenia was a stupid tiny kingdom. She didn't understand why her father was doing this.

Another song was about to start and she hoped with all her heart that someone other than the prince would ask her to dance. A hand was extended to her. She looked up and saw Sian. As much as she disliked him, she felt happy, wondering if Darian had sent him.

They walked to the dance floor. When she was sure

nobody could hear them, she asked, "Have you seen your brother?"

"Not yet. It's been only three months. I don't want anyone to suspect I helped him."

Helped him. How *dare* he? But she decided to comment on that. "So you don't have any news?"

"Why? Do you happen to care if he lives or dies? I doubt it. I warned you and you didn't care. You didn't care if there was any danger, and didn't care to check, as long as you had a puppy to play with."

Cayla rolled her eyes. "I had to say that. I was trying to save his life."

"Not sure if you noticed, but I'm the one who saved his life."

"Oh, after you had him imprisoned and almost killed? How noble of you."

"I wasn't expecting thanks, you know. But you do realize I risked my life, my position, my rank, everything, for my brother. Why would I have planned it?"

"Because you knew you could get everything you wanted. Darian was sent away. You came out a hero. But I see through you."

"Right. I planned to fight an experienced soldier."

"That fight was a joke. You were pretending the entire time."

He raised an eyebrow. "Impressive. And how do you know that?"

"I was hidden, but I watched the audience and observed your footwork. I know fighting techniques."

"True. I saw you training with my brother."

Cayla stopped and stared at him. She wished she could slap him, punch him, something.

"What? I don't see anything offensive in what I just said. If anything, I might be the only person who didn't draw wrong conclusions about you two on the ground."

Cayla sighed. Maybe he was right. Sian was annoying because she never knew when he was being sarcastic or just saying the truth. She looked at him. "I still think you planned it."

"I am a good strategist, I'll give you that. But no matter what you say, *you* are the one who kept seeing him and didn't care. Accusing me won't wash away your guilt, girl."

"And acting outraged won't make me change my mind about you. Is that what you wanted to tell me?"

"No. I might see my brother in a couple weeks and I want to know what to tell him."

"You don't have to tell him anything."

Sian had a smug, unpleasant smile. "Oh, but I must. I noticed the smiles and favors you give the Arlenia prince. I noticed how often you danced. I'm not stupid."

How dare he? As if it was her fault. Cayla rolled her eyes. "If you think I was smiling at the prince, you need to have your eyes checked."

"I'll be straightforward with you then: don't break my brother's heart. He's young and innocent. I know you were just using him to pass the time. And now you turned your attention to the prince."

"You're disgusting, Sian. Tell your brother whatever you want. You've always wanted to break us apart. But he'll know what you're trying to do. And he'll know you were the one who meddled."

Darian would know how she felt and his stupid brother wasn't going to break them apart. Or so she hoped.

"Well, he'll know you're fickle, and that you were bound to disappoint him. Love is poison. That's what women do, isn't it?"

Cayla laughed. "Why—disappointed that no girl loves you?"

"That would be impossible. I can't be disappointed in what I don't expect."

She laughed again. "At least you're realistic. That's one good quality."

"That's a great quality. I am realistic—and rational—but my brother isn't, and I won't forgive you for what you did."

"I won't forgive you either, Sian. Does that make us even? I wonder how you'll talk to me when I'm queen."

"Queen of tiny Arlenia? How wonderful."

"Queen of Whyland, you stupid. Did you forget who I am? Is that why you hate your brother—you're jealous he'll marry the queen?"

"Marry? I wasn't told about the engagement. But if you're serious about it, maybe you should reconsider the attention you've been giving to the prince. I see the way you look at each other."

"The way he looks at me. It's not my fault."

"You didn't seem too bothered."

"Sian, you're being disgusting and making false assumptions. I'll make a formal complaint against you if you continue."

"You're going to make up lies against me? Like you did against my brother?"

"I didn't. Stop it."

"I'll stop. The music is almost over anyways. Do you want me to tell my brother anything?"

"No."

"So you just don't care."

"I don't care what you say, that's all."

The music stopped and Cayla walked outside. She hated Sian, but he wasn't completely wrong. She had been careless and almost caused Darian's death. Now he was away with the army, in a dangerous region, risking death again. But then she knew it had been Sian's fault. And how dare he mention the prince? She hated him. She wished she could remain in her bedroom. But she needed to obey her father. At least for now. But she was tired of being told what to do, of being confined within the castle walls. She wanted to scream, run, but she couldn't. Her hands touched the place where Darian's twin necklace should be. She missed it. It was the one thing that brought her comfort.

She worried what Sian would say, though. Would he make up lies about her? Would Darian be jealous? But he'd never been jealous. She wished she could be with him, but knew she had to be patient. It was one of the reasons she didn't want to contradict her father. Maybe one day he'd understand. Maybe he'd allow them to see each other again. She was hopeful. But for now, she had to wait.

Cayla was also afraid of contacting Darian while inside the castle. It had something that blocked the necklace, so she had to go to the gardens. Still, she had the odd feeling she was being followed and that her gardens were no longer safe. She didn't want anyone to know what her necklace could do, and to know she'd contacted Darian. It could cost him his life. She would never put his life at risk again. She closed her eyes. She had to wait.

Odell had been telling her she would need to defeat Lylah, that it was her duty. She lived in a castle on an island on the Black River. Cayla would defeat her, and would gain her father's trust. That would mean freedom. And there was something else as well: she'd need to leave the castle to defeat Lylah. She imagined herself stepping out into the world and tasting freedom. Meanwhile, all she had to do was be patient and wait, and shut down the desire to run away and scream.

10

DARIAN'S RESOLUTIONS

Darian watched the flames grow as the village burned. He wondered how many stories and memories were being consumed by the fire. Favorite chairs, favorite books, pans that had cooked many meals, toys, cribs… All lost. But he showed no emotion. At least the villagers were safe. They had been warned the previous night and escaped before commander Sarris could find and question them. As revenge, their village was set on fire.

Darian watched, thinking about his own village, and that one day the army might find it and burn it down just like this one. At least if they were alive they could rebuild.

Sarris laughed. He had some sadistic pleasure in seeing people suffer.

In the last three months, Darian had learned what the army did in the South; they destroyed and killed. He'd spoken to his father about it, and unfortunately wasn't surprised to learn that Keen supported these tactics. His father believed the people were assembling against the king and the army in support of Lylah, and that it was their duty to rid the kingdom of any act of disobedience. But the list of acts of disobedience was huge and illogical. More and more members of the army were deserting at the risk of being killed. Darian didn't desert. He wanted to use his position to do good and he was doing it.

While before, there were people organized here and there against the king, this time they could join their efforts for a great uprising. Darian was just with a battalion for now, but hoped he'd have the chance to go back to Siphoria to the communication center. From there, he could coordinate these different groups. When he met dissatisfied members of the army, he spoke to them. They were forming an alliance within its ranks to take power from within. There was a lot of work ahead of them, but he was sure they would be able to achieve their goals. These thoughts made him feel less guilty for standing alongside war criminals.

SARRIS, Darian, and seven other soldiers walked back to the encampment. Darian did his best to seem satisfied and relaxed as if he'd enjoyed destroying innocent people's homes. As they walked among the trees, he suddenly felt a sharp pain in his left arm, and a little blood started dripping. It was a dart. A little blood was dripping from the puncture. He knew what was happening; the villagers hadn't run but were rather ambushing them. A few more well-placed shots could do a great deal of damage. Maybe they could even kill Sarris. But with superior weapons, the odds were in the army's favor. Those villagers would be slaughtered.

Darian looked down, hoping nobody had noticed it, when another soldier yelled, "We're under attack! Ready all weapons!"

The soldiers formed a circle, standing back to back, but they didn't see anyone. Darian looked up and saw a human figure on one of the trees. It was a boy, no more than thirteen. His eyes met the boy's eyes, which were filled with fear. Darian looked away, hoping nobody else had seen him, hoping the boy could escape. A loud noise squashed Darian's hopes. The boy's small body fell on the ground.

Everything around Darian blurred. Sounds and images stopped making sense. All he felt was cold dread and guilt. The boy could have been Darian not long before, fighting for freedom, defending his people, daring, hopeful, brave. Now he was gone. Everything turned black.

Darian woke up in Sarris' lift. His arm was bandaged, but the surrounding skin looked blue and purple.

"We called a doctor from Siphoria," Sarris said. "You were poisoned, son."

Son. That word gave Darian shivers. He knew it was just an expression, but it reminded him of how much he was related to all that was cruel and unfair in his kingdom.

Sarris continued, "Your brother and father might come by, for a farewell."

Farewell? Darian looked at his arm. The poison was spreading. He knew there was a solution. "Can't we cut off the arm?"

"Your father forbids it. And the poison has already spread."

Darian couldn't believe it. Was it that his father didn't want a lame son? Maybe he should try to cut off his own arm—he wanted to live–but he didn't say any of that. He only asked, "Why have a doctor then?"

"We need to identify the poison." He looked at Darian. "I'm sorry, but that's the price of war. At least you'll die in peace knowing you were fighting to defend your kingdom from rebellion and disobedience."

Darian swallowed hard. He couldn't come to terms with the news. Dying? But he was so young. He hadn't even started everything he planned. He hadn't seen the king defeated. It couldn't be. How ironic that he, the only one who had tried to defend the village, would be the one to die. The price of war. But no. He was going to fight. He was going to find a solution. Sarris might have given him up for dead, but Darian wasn't going to simply lie down and wait for death to take him.

He got up and asked, "Permission to go for a walk?"

Sarris shook his head. "Not in your state."

"It might be my last time."

The old commander exhaled and said, "Go. But come back."

Darian walked outside. His colleagues were sitting in a circle and didn't notice him. He walked to the woods. There, he removed the bandage and cleaned up the thick balm from the wound. He saw the place he had been punctured, cut the skin around it, and rebandaged it. Darian had no idea what the poison could be—they didn't have that stuff in the village he'd grown up in—but he knew the best place to find an antidote was with the poison makers. He walked hoping to find someone, hoping they'd know he was not on the army's side. He had some idea of where the villagers had gone. The hills. He gathered all his strength to walk in that direction. Before he went much farther, he fainted again.

DARIAN WASN'T sure if he was dreaming or awake. He lay on a pile of hay in a cave while two women took care of him. They had blond hair and blue eyes like Nia, the king's wife. He heard fragments of conversations, and couldn't quite be sure who said what or if it was his imagination.

"And what if he can't stand it?" one said.

"Look at his necklace. He's from the lost people in the North."

"He doesn't seem to have learned any magic."

"It might be for the best. His path is different."

"His magic might be amplified with this."

"If it is, it will help him. It will help us as well."

"What is his magic?"

"I saw him when he convinced the village leaders. He's a whisperer."

"Spell speaker."

"What?"

"They call them spell speakers in the North. If he is one, he'll become even more powerful."

"Should we allow a boy to have such power? We could let him die."

"We found him. There's a reason. If we turn away now, we'll be murderers. And he's one of the lost people."

"But he's a boy."

"But he doesn't know about his magic and he'll never have the training. He'll just be a natural leader. If he wants to bring down the army, it will help him, and help us."

DARIAN WOKE in the same place he had fainted, in the woods, not far away from the lifts. His arm wasn't bandaged and there was a scar where he had carved it. He started to think the conversation he'd heard had been real. The women had cured him. It was day, but he had no idea how much time had passed. Days? Months? He walked back to the encampment. The lifts were still there. Nobody was outside. He went into Sarris' lift. The old man sat at a table, reading.

He barely raised his eyes. "Enjoyed the walk?"

"Very much. I feel a lot better."

"The doctor should be here soon."

THE DOCTOR LOOKED at Darian's arm in disbelief.

"How was this cured?"

Darian shrugged. "I don't know. Maybe it wasn't as bad as we thought."

The man looked at him with an air of understanding. "Few people can cure that type of poison." He then whispered in Darian's ear. "Please help us make sure they don't all get killed."

The doctor's name was Jonathan. He became one more person to add to Darian's list of contacts—people who were resisting the king and fighting for freedom however they could.

A PRIVATE LIFT landed near the encampment. Sarris went to greet the newcomer with such a fuss one would think he was going to greet the king himself. It wasn't the king. It was only Sian. Despite being only sixteen, he walked side by side with Sarris, smiling and charming the commander, who acted with a deference that would be odd if it wasn't for the way Sian ported himself. He did act like a king.

Darian then remembered his dream, delirious visions, or memories from when he was cured. "He's a whisperer. A spell speaker." He had no idea what a whisperer or spell speaker was, but he remembered his mother speaking with a hypnotic voice, and remembered how his brother had done the same in Darian's audience. While the women might have suspected Darian was one, he was sure his brother was the one with the real power there. He wished his brother could use it for good, but wasn't so sure, as he watched Sian and Sarris walking side by side and tapping each other's shoulders like very old friends, with satisfied smiles at seeing each other.

Sian saw Darian, but didn't pay him much attention and took his time talking to the old commander before walking over to him. with extended arms and an air of surprise. "Back from the dead again! I can't believe I have such an immortal brother."

"Upset?"

"Don't be weird, little brother. I came as fast as I could, didn't I? Let's walk a little."

The two brothers started walking away from the encampment.

Darian said, "You seemed more interested in talking to Sarris."

He laughed. "Are you jealous? I'm flattered. But consider that I didn't risk my life to save him."

Darian remembered the duel, the audience, and how his brother had stepped up for him. He also remembered his brother's warnings and the feeling that he had been involved in the accusations brought against him. Still, he didn't want to argue about it. "Well, thanks."

Sian stopped and put his hands on his heart as if he was about to have an attack. "Wait, wait, wait. What did you say?"

His brother was weird sometimes. Still, Darian repeated it. "Thanks."

Sian made an exaggerated expression of disbelief. "No, that can't be real. My ears are playing tricks on me. Are you sure you want to thank me for something? Are you feeling well? Maybe the poison has affected your sanity."

Darian rolled his eyes. "Yeah, maybe that's it."

"Most definitely. Cause my normal brother Darian would find something to complain about."

"Well, you did extend the fight too much. You even got hurt. Why didn't you just finish Lalus sooner?"

"Of course. Killing is so easy, isn't it?" Sian looked down. "But I had no choice. Either way, the thing is, when you're good at something, you don't want your enemies to know it. And the king wanted a spectacle." His voice lowered. "I gave him one."

"How is your shoulder?"

"Cured. How is your arm?"

Darian shrugged. "It's cured as well. I think Sarris made a mistake when he thought I was poisoned."

"We get a lot of training in first aid, poison symptoms, and how to cure the most common wounds. You would have known if you'd stayed in the academy. I don't think Sarris would make such a mistake."

"What are you suggesting?"

"There's something you're hiding, little brother." Sian looked at him. "I know it, but I won't tell anyone. You're free to complain about it, as always, of course."

Darian shook his head. He didn't want to argue with Sian. In fact, what he most wanted was for his brother to help him. He knew that if he and his brother united forces, they could defeat the king and their father quickly and easily, but he wasn't sure where his brother's loyalties stood. He tried to find out.

"Have you heard about the uprising movement?"

Sian nodded. "I also came to warn you about it." He

looked around, probably to make sure they were not being overheard. "This movement, it's not a movement. It's a bunch of different people and groups with various ideologies. They'll never be completely united. If by chance they rise to power, Whyland will plunge into chaos. So please pay attention to that, my brother."

"So you think we should support the army? Do you have any idea what they've been doing?"

"We need to take control of the army. Once it's done, we can change it. It's possible. Look at Siphoria. I'm in control of the city. Go there and see. But you need to take control first. You need to move *within* the established power, not topple it. You can't predict what will happen if the power changes hands too suddenly."

"And what's your idea?"

"Gaining power and influence over the army. That's what I've been doing. Now, I'll be honest here. I know what you are planning on doing. If you support these rebels, this uprising, you'll get a knife on your back. And I'll tell you more: I'll protect you as much as I can, but eventually we'll be on opposite sides."

"So you want to fight the uprising?"

"Not necessarily. In life, we must be strategic. But please be aware that at the end of the day, it's about power, not freedom or any other noble ideologies."

"For you, maybe."

"I won't insist on it. But come and talk to me when you're ready to support me."

"And you're going to be supported by people like Sarris?"

Sian shrugged. "I'm not picky about my friends, you see?"

"If your stomach doesn't curl, then you have a problem."

"Maybe I do. It's pretty to be noble and idealistic, but you cannot do anything without power. That's the fact."

"The world has more power than a few men commanding weapons."

"Of course. I never said I was picky. We're not going to agree, are we?"

"I'm afraid not."

"You want to support rebels, support them. But I won't save you this time."

Darian wasn't sure if it was a warning or a threat. He had to be cautious. "I'm not supporting anybody. I'm just trying to survive."

Sian smiled. "Of course. Survive your way. I'll survive mine. I had something else to tell you."

"What is it?"

"Cayla." Sian's worried expression knotted Darian's stomach. "Do you know that the prince of Arlenia has been courting her?"

Darian didn't know why his brother was bringing it up. "I heard something about it—why?"

"Well, at the last ball, they danced all night, and she gave him a lot of attention. Then they both disappeared."

"What are you suggesting?"

"I'm not suggesting anything. I'm telling what I saw. I assumed you'd want to know what she does when you're not around."

Darian wasn't sure what his brother wanted, but it

couldn't be anything good. He shook his head. "Just do me a favor, will you? Don't follow Cayla, and don't make assumptions about what she is or isn't doing. I'm sure she'll let me know if she's fallen in love with someone else."

Sian laughed. "With someone else. Look at your confidence."

"Jealous you can't trust anyone's love?"

"Love is poison, brother, but if you're so sure about Cayla's love, I won't worry about it. But don't complain if she makes a fool out of you."

"If you came here to offend her, I'm going to ask you to leave."

"I was leaving anyways." Sian turned around, then stopped and looked back at his brother. "Traitor."

Darian watched as his brother walked away. Darian felt sad that they were parting ways and going in different directions. His brother lusted for power. He wasn't a bad person, but he was proud and ambitious. Maybe he'd see Darian's side one day.

Darian then pulled his necklace from under his shirt. It shone. He knew Cayla wouldn't contact him anytime soon, and it was for the best. He'd stopped thinking about her, but not because he liked her any less, but because he was focused now.

He would help the rebels and the king would be deposed. As much as he knew Cayla would feel hurt and even betrayed, Darian knew it was for the best. For Cayla, for the memory of the brave young boy who tried to kill him, for the memory of the unknown women who had saved him, for the villagers who had lost everything, for his mother, Darian would dedicate each and every second of his life to the uprising. He would work from within the army to establish alliances. He would use his father's influence to take charge of the communication center. He knew they would win. He could taste victory and envisioned a new era in Whyland.

IF YOU WANT to know how the story continues, check *Step Into Magic* on Amazon at https://amzn.to/2Jwo7Wx

You can also jump straight into *Kissing Magic* at mybook.to/KissingMagic

ABOUT THE AUTHOR

I'm originally from Brazil, I live in Montreal with my son and I love to create worlds and characters.

You can learn more about me and keep in touch at dayleitao.com! Don't forget to sign up for my newsletter so you know when I release the next book.

Thanks very much for reading. You make it all be worth it!